Mr. Undeniable

One Scorching Summer, Volume 3

Lori Wilde

Published by Lori Wilde, 2023.

MR. UNDENIABLE

First edition. April 11, 2023.

Copyright © 2023 Lori Wilde.

ISBN: 979-8215197998

Written by Lori Wilde.

Table of Contents

Chapter 1

S ex had never looked so intriguing...
      Or so scary.

Which was precisely the point. Jorgina Gerard needed to step far outside her comfort zone and get a life.

She closed the glossy brochure, featuring Eros Airlines and Fantasy Resort Erotic Vacation packages, and fanned herself, alarmed that her body was suddenly aroused at, of all places, the Dallas/Fort Worth International Airport ticket kiosk. Mentally, she shook herself. What was the matter with her?

Um, maybe it was because she hadn't had sex since her boyfriend dumped her six months ago.

Cringing, Jorgie bit down on her bottom lip.

All around her there was bustling activity as business travelers rolled their carry-on bags toward the taxi stands, lovers reunited with heartfelt hugs, harried moms and dads herded ebullient children from the enticing dangers of escalators and baggage carousels.

What was she doing? Why had she let her best friend since kindergarten, Avery Bodel, talk her into this? Was she insane? Embarking on an exotic itinerary dubbed with the provocative title *Make Love Like a Courtesan*.

She didn't need sex lessons. She was twenty-five. She'd been in a long-term relationship and... and...

And as Brian had walked out the door, he'd tossed over his shoulder. "You're just too damned boring in the bed, Jorgina. Too conventional by half. I need variety, excitement, *danger*..."

Danger?

Jorgie closed her eyes and took a deep breath. Maybe she wasn't the problem, maybe it was Brian and if Brian was the problem, then she didn't need to be here, right? She just needed to find some guy who could appreciate her for who she was. The urge to flee before she got in over her head, beset her.

"You know, on second thought..." She turned to her friend.

This week, Avery's hair was dyed the color of muscat grapes, a deep hue of electric purple. As a hairdresser, Avery changed her hairstyle and color as often as most people changed clothes.

"Yes?" Avery arched an eyebrow.

"Maybe this—"

"Oh, no." Avery wrapped a restraining hand around Jorgie's wrist. "You are *not* backing out!"

"Not what?" Jorgie's voice came out high and squeaky, giving her away.

"You're not fooling me. I've known you too long. You've got that I'm-gonna-run-away-from-fun look in your eyes. The same look you had in eighth grade when we played Spin The Bottle at Miley Kinslow's birthday party and it pointed to the guy you'd been mooning over and instead of kissing him, you hopped up and hid in the closet. Remember that?"

"Quint Mason," Jorgie said. "And everyone laughed at me."

She'd had a puppy-love crush on Quint for the entire school year, and he barely knew she existed. If she squeezed her eyes closed tightly enough, she could still see him as he'd looked then—tall, lanky, medium brown hair, a devilish grin that melted tweenaged hearts.

Of course, as a tenth grader, he'd never given her the time of day, and she'd been far too shy to even say boo to him, but she'd been besotted. Jorgie sighed. She'd been getting it wrong with the opposite sex ever since.

She wondered whatever happened to Quint. Then she remembered something her brother Keith had told her in passing after his ten-year high school reunion the previous fall where he'd and Quint had chatted. Quint had been stationed in Afghanistan, but that he'd recently left the Air Force and was working for some private airline.

"Yeah." Avery tapped her temple with an index finger. "Quint Mason. That's him. This trip is just like that. Instead of hiding in the closet, you have the chance to grab life by the throat and really live."

"But is an erotically themed destination vacation really the answer?"

"Look at this." Avery snatched the Eros brochure from her hand and shook it under her nose. "Look at all the opportunities you'd be running away from."

Jorgie sighed. "I guess."

Her friend flipped through the pages, reading the ad copy out loud. "Learn the sex secrets every courtesan knew. Find out how to hold men completely in your thrall. Dance the seductive dance that brought kings to their knees. Become a woman of exotic pleasures."

Embarrassment heated Jorgie's cheeks. She snatched the brochure back and stuffed it inside her purse. "Shh, someone will hear you."

Avery shrugged. "So what? I'm not ashamed."

"There are kids around."

"Hey, I'm not their mother. It's not my job to censor their exposure to the world."

"Maybe not, but you don't have to announce to the entire airport where we're going."

"Seriously," Avery said, "don't run away. This is your chance to show that dork, Brian, that you're anything but boring, and where does he get off accusing you of being too conventional? You two met at an accountants' conference, for crying out loud. He's just as conventional as you, or he was before he—"

"But I *am* conventional."

"Conventional is as conventional does."

"Huh?"

"It's something my Grammie says."

"Your Grammie says, 'conventional is as conventional does'?"

"No, she says 'pretty is as pretty does,' I just substituted conventional, but the advice still applies."

"Huh?"

"Sure, it does. Act pretty and you'll be pretty. Act conventional and you'll be conventional. Act unconventional and—"

"I get your drift."

"Stop dragging your feet. Actually, stop thinking. You think too much, Jorgie."

"And you never look before you leap, Avery."

"But I have a lot more fun than you do."

True enough. "You know, this is just a variation of the same conversation we've been having for twenty years."

"I'm the accelerator..." Avery said, starting the quote their mothers who'd spoken over their heads as they'd played in the sandbox together. Avery was the kid who flung herself headfirst down the slide. While Jorgie was the crying girl who hovered on the top rung of the ladder, too scared to climb back down, too fearful to take the plunge.

"And I'm the brake," Jorgie finished.

"We balance each other out. It's the secret to our lifelong friendship." Grinning, Avery slung her arm over Jorgie's shoulder.

Avery's grin bolstered her sagging confidence. Truthfully, she didn't know what she'd do without her friend. Avery had such a strong life force. Whenever she was around her, Jorgie instantly felt stronger, braver, more adventuresome. What few risks Jorgie had taken were due solely to her best friend's influence. Avery was an exuberant leader, barreling her way through life on magnetic charm and sheer good luck.

"Your turn." Avery elbowed her forward.

Shoulder muscles tensed tight as a wire, Jorgie stepped up to the kiosk and inserted her credit card. Ready or not, this was happening.

"While you're doing that," Avery told her, "I'm going to the ticket counter."

"Huh? What for?"

"Never you mind. I'll be right back." Avery raised her hand over her head and gave Jorgie a backward wave.

Her friend sashayed over to the ticket counter, her low-rise jeans and cropped cotton T-shirt revealing a peek at the vivid ink art decorating her lower spine. Jorgie would never ever have the courage to get a tattoo, but as much as Avery's audacity shocked her, she also admired her friend's bravery.

The ticket kiosk spit out Jorgie's boarding pass.

It was confirmed. She and Avery were on their way to Venice to learn how to make love like courtesans. Not that Avery needed sex lessons—the woman kept more men dangling on the string than she could count—but her friend could definitely do with a dose of the courtesans' famed discretion.

Okay, all right, she would do this. She needed this. It was time she stopped playing it safe. Brian was right. She *was* too conventional. She could do this as long as she had Avery beside her.

Speaking of Avery, where in the heck had she gotten off to?

Ticket in one hand and her carry-on clasped in the other, Jorgie spun away from the kiosk. She was so busy searching the crowd for her friend that she didn't see the man barreling down on her until it was too late. She tried to zigzag, but that only made things worse because he did the same thing.

Wham!

They collided in a tangle of arms and legs and rolling luggage on the floor together.

"Are you okay?" His voice was as deep as Phantom Lake, where her parents owned a summer cottage.

His hands rested on her shoulders, steadying her. Jorgie lay on the floor and her skirt had flipped up, revealing way too much thigh. She yanked her skirt to her knees and darted her gaze to his face.

Had he noticed?

His teasing grin said it all. Oh yeah, he'd noticed.

And she was noticing for the first time just how extremely handsome he was. The stuff of daydreams. Chiseled jaw. Neatly trimmed thick, wavy brown hair. Mischievous cocoa-colored eyes. A slightly crooked nose that told her it had been broken at one time, but it kept him from being too damned gorgeous.

She felt like fleeing. Jorgie gulped, stared. *Say something, dummy.*

"Hey," he said. "I know you."

She frowned, shook her head, unable to speak against the weight of his warm, distracting hand on her shoulder.

"Yeah, yeah, sure I do. I used to hang out with your brother Keith when my family lived in Burleson. It's Quint, Quint Mason. Remember me?" He extended a hand.

Quint Mason? Was it possible? Here? Now? She stared, stunned by coincidence and his absolute gorgeousness.

His hand stayed outstretched; the smile firmly hung on his lips.

She almost laughed. Not because there was anything funny, but to help relieve her nervous tension. What else could she do?

His hand was hard but friendly, just like the man himself. He had a look of surprised delight on his face, and she could hardly believe he was that glad to see her. Gently, he tugged her to her feet.

She felt oddly absurd, as if she'd stumbled down an *Alice in Wonderland* rabbit hole. A really cool rabbit hole, yes, but an odd sensation all the same. "Umm... umm..."

"How have you been, Jorgie?" he asked, his voice low and warm.

Yikes! Her heart was on fire. He'd remembered her name! Her name on his tongue felt as tender as a hug.

"Wow, you've certainly changed." An appreciative light danced in his eyes.

She wasn't the only one who'd changed. He'd gone from lean and lanky to muscular and broad-shouldered. From good-looking to drop-dead handsome.

"No more braces." He tapped his front teeth.

Her body flushed hot. "I got them off when I was a sophomore."

"No more pigtails." His hand went to her hair, his fingertips briefly skimming her neck.

Goose bumps set up camp on her forearms, and her breathing grew so shallow she was practically panting. "Left those behind with the private school uniform."

"And you don't have library books clutched in your arms. Did you still love reading?"

"I adore it. Nothing's changed there, but I've upgraded to an e-book reader. Got it stashed in my purse for the plane ride."

"And you aren't wearing glasses."

"I got LASIK," she said.

"Those beautiful eyes are the same." He nodded. "So deep blue that they're almost purple. Like a Colorado mountain stream. Few people have eyes that color, but the minute I looked into yours, I knew it was you."

He remembered her!

She shouldn't have found the idea so damn thrilling, but she did. Her junior high crush remembered her! Her heart did a crazy little rumba and all those old memories of yearning and burning squeezed her chest tight.

Calm down, Jorgina. You're getting overexcited.

"You know," he said. "I'd love to grab a drink, and catch up on old times..."

What old times? She hadn't spoken to him ten times the entire year he'd lived in Burleson and hung out with her brother. She'd been far too shy. Far too gobsmacked by such a self-confident guy.

"But..." He glanced at his watch. "I'm late for work. Maybe we could hook up when you get back home?" His comment had been mildly made, but it threw her off to think of meeting up with him again.

"Maybe." She breathed, hopeful even as her brain churned with a thousand reasons why that was a bad idea.

He pulled a business card from the pocket of his sport jacket, he just had to be a snazzy dresser, as well as good-looking, and passed it over to her. "Call me when you get back in town."

Yeah, right. She'd find the courage to do that about the same time hell froze over. Still, she palmed the card and clutched it tight.

"See ya." He picked up his carry-on, raised a hand in farewell, and took off.

Stunned, Jorgie felt as if she'd been clipped in a drive-by. What was this odd sensation?

Avery sidled up. "Omigod, who's the hottie?"

Simultaneously, they both cocked their heads to watch Quint walk away, the fabric of his slacks molding to his toned butt. They sighed in unison.

"That," Jorgie said, "was Quint Mason."

"Quint Mason of Spin The Bottle fame? Get outta town." Avery gave her a playful shove.

Jorgie pointed to her luggage. "I'm working on it."

Avery giggled. "You know what I mean. This is incredible."

"How so?"

"It's kismet, fate, serendipity, manifest destiny. I mean, we were just talking about Quint and *poof*...here he was. What are the odds?"

"Well, actually," Jorgie said, her mathematical accountant's mind kicking in, "the probability isn't as slim as you might think, given that Quint works in the airline industry and DFW is the biggest airport in the state. He probably passes through here every morning on his way to work."

"Yeah, but what are the odds that you'd be standing here when he sauntered by?"

"I could do a statistical analysis if you wanted..."

Avery plastered her palms over both ears. "No, no, please spare me. Numbers make my head explode."

"It's really just like that phenomena where you decide to buy a certain car—"

"Porsche. I want a Porsche Boxster."

"You decide to buy a Porsche Boxster," Jorgie said, "and suddenly everywhere you look is crawling with Porsches Boxsters. Baader-Meinhof."

"Huh?"

"That's what the phenomena is called. Baader-Meinhof syndrome. It's named after—"

Avery raised a hand. "Don't need the blow by blow, thanks. You just can't resist anything brainiac-ish, can you."

"Anyway, if we hadn't been talking about Quint, then I probably would never have noticed him. He would have walked right on by. Just like if you weren't dying to own a Porsche Boxster, you wouldn't notice every single one of them that drove past."

"Except that Quint didn't walk right on by, did he? The man ran smack-dab into you."

"You saw that?"

"The whole airport saw it."

Jorgie winced. She hated being the center of attention. Unlike Avery, who courted the spotlight with glee, although Jorgie did admire her friend's brazenness.

"Don't obsess about it," Avery said. "No one cares that your skirt was practically up around your waist."

Jorgie groaned.

"Look at the bright side. At least you weren't going commando. Come on. Let's get through security before the line gets any longer. Our plane boards in fifteen minutes."

Avery was right. No point obsessing over something she couldn't change. She needed to live in the moment and get fired up about her trip. She was going to Venice! What more could a woman ask for?

By the time they were through the checkpoint and found their gate at Eros Air, boarding was already in progress.

"Hey," Avery said, nudging Jorgie in the side. "Isn't that him?"

"Who?"

"Mr. Handsome over there by the gate attendant."

Jorgie focused on the jetway. Sure enough, Quint Mason getting on the plane. *Her* plane. To Venice. What was he doing on her plane?

Quint had said he was late for work. Did he work for Eros? Was he a pilot, or a navigator, or a flight attendant? But he wasn't in uniform.

Jorgie frowned and looked at her ticket. "Are we at the right gate?"

"E37. That's you."

She focused back on Avery. "What do you mean, that's me?"

"This is your gate."

"My gate?" She raised an eyebrow.

Avery shifted her weight. "My gate's at E34."

"Your gate?" Jorgie blinked, not understanding.

"I decided at the last minute I'd rather go on the Make Love Like A Movie Star tour. I'm headed for LaLa Land while you're jetting off to the City of Canals."

Stunned, Jorgie felt her jaw dropped. "Huh?"

"I'm going to Hollywood and you're going to Venice."

"That's what you were doing at the ticket counter? Changing your destination?"

Avery gave her a don't-hate-me smile. "Yes."

"And they just let you switch like that?"

"I had to pay a fee, but yeah."

Jorgie felt as if she'd been slapped across the face. "What's going on? Why didn't you tell me? I would be just as happy going on the movie star tour. Let's go back and swap my ticket, too."

"Um, I kinda, sorta want to go alone."

Dismay sucked all the joy out of her. "But... but... This whole Eros vacation was your idea. You told me to spread my wings, to claim my sexuality, and show Brian that I could be as unconventional as...as...a Venetian courtesan."

Avery placed a hand on Jorgie's shoulder. "And that's what you're going to do."

"Not without you I'm not."

"Jorg, we've gotta cut the cord sometime. I can't keep being your id. You gotta develop your own sense of fun."

"Well, that sounds all great and everything," Jorgie said, still hurt by the turn of events. She'd never expected Avery to pull something like this. Sure, her friend was spontaneous and free-spirited, and okay, she could be irresponsible, but she'd never betrayed Jorgie before. "But who's going to be your brake?"

"That's just it. This time, I wanna freefall, no brakes, no parachutes, nothing to hold me back."

"I...I... never knew you felt this way. I thought we balanced each other out. I thought that was why our friendship worked so well."

"Listen, it's not the end of the world," Avery said in a perky voice, as if she wasn't about to cut the cord with a pair of giant metaphorical scissors. "We're simply taking separate vacations. We're still BFFs."

"I would never have agreed to the trip if I'd known you were going to bail on me." Jorgie fisted her hands.

"I know." Avery gave her a gentle, it's-for-your-own-good smile. "It's the reason I did it this way. I hope you'll forgive me."

Betrayal had an ugly taste, bitter and sour. "Don't do this. You can switch your ticket back. I'll pay the fee. Please."

"Time to pull up your big-girl panties, Jorgie." Avery hoisted her knapsack onto her shoulder. "Ciao."

"You can't... You're not... Avery, don't leave me."

"You depend too much on me, kiddo."

Her friend was right. She sounded so desperate. She felt desperate, too. Her life had been unraveling ever since Brian left her and now Avery was leaving her, too.

"Please..."

"You can do this. I have faith. We'll call each other every day and share our experiences."

"Ave..." Jorgie was finding it hard to breathe.

Tumultuous emotions clogged her lungs—betrayal, anger, and strangely enough, excitement. She'd never done anything on her own. She and Avery had roomed together in college, and then afterward she'd met Brian and they'd moved in together and then, after Brian left, she got another roommate.

"Final boarding call for Eros Air flight 692," said a voice over the loudspeaker.

"Go on." Avery gave her a gentle shove toward the jetway. "This is for your own good."

"Please, don't make me do this!"

"Spread your wings, Jorgie, flout convention, fly, go to your destiny." With that parting advice, Avery turned and scurried away.

Quickly, the crowd swallowed her up.

Jorgie stood frozen, her heart pounding madly. The gate agent looked at her expectantly, hand outstretched to receive her boarding pass.

She locked eyes with the woman and the life-changing events of the past year washed over her. Getting dumped by

Brian for being too timid, getting passed over for a promotion at work because she wasn't aggressive enough (a direct quote from her boss), the decision to take Avery's advice and sign up for an erotic fantasy vacation, unexpectedly meeting Quint Mason and then discovering he was on her flight.

Was it kismet? Was serendipity at work here? Had the universe converged to plant her in this spot under these conditions for a reason?

Jorgie wasn't fanciful. She was an accountant. A cruncher of numbers. She liked things that made sense, and this romantic notion of destiny defied logic. And yet, here she was with the cosmic dominoes all lined up. Did she have the courage to knock them down?

"Miss?" the gate agent asked. "Are you boarding?"

It was now or never. Time to prove she could be bold and daring, or forever accept her fate as a shy, conventional woman who could never attract the attention of someone like, say... Quint Mason.

Jorgie raised her chin and slapped her ticket into the gate agent's hand. "Yes," she said. "Yes, I am."

Chapter 2

Well, well, well, little Jorgie Gerard had grown up quite nicely.

From his seat in the back of the plane. Quint Mason watched Jorgie board the Eros Air Bombardier CRJ200.

She moved up the aisle, her carry-on bag clutched in her hand, her gorgeous blue eyes bright, her movements lithe and graceful.

Simply gorgeous.

Quint couldn't believe how stunning Jorgie had become. He had always thought of her as a kid sister, but now, he couldn't help but feel a deep attraction towards her.

As she made her way farther down the aisle, he followed her with his eyes. His gaze tripping lightly over her lush curves. She hadn't possessed a body like that thirteen years ago.

Spellbound, he simply stared.

The front of her silky, powder-blue blouse dipped, revealing a hint of cleavage, just enough to cause instant sweat to bead on the back of his neck. She stopped a few rows ahead of him and looked down to double-check her seat assignment, and then she glanced up again. Using a paper boarding pass instead of her cell phone pegged her as a novice flyer.

A ray of sunshine slanted through the open portal window, casting her in a surreal splash of soft yellow glow For a whisper of a second, he could have sworn he heard harp music and the sound of angels singing. The woman who used to be his best friend's shy little sister was bathed in a whole new light.

Her straight, chestnut-brown hair—swept back off her neck in a demure ponytail—glinted with red highlights. His fingers itched to reach up and pull that band from her hair and watch it tumble about her shoulders. She wore a knee-length skirt that was a darker shade of blue than her blouse and blue, matching sandals decorated with pink flowers. She looked like exactly what she was, the girl-next-door all grown up. Jorgina was the woman you took home to meet the parents.

Marriage material.

He'd do well to steer clear of her, but even as the light shifted and dimmed, Quint couldn't take his eyes off her and, for the life of him, he didn't know why.

Familiarity?

She reminded him of a simpler time. That's all it was. A blast from the past. Still, his heart skipped a beat. That was odd. Usually the only time his heart misfired was when he drove his Corvette too fast or danced the two-step or made love all night long. She was beautiful, hell yeah, but certainly nothing extraordinary.

Nothing to make him feel like *this*.

But there was something about the self-contained way she carried herself that clutched his gut and narrowed his focus to only her. She possessed a quiet quality that called to something primal inside him. Then one dominate thought snapped through his head, hot as electricity.

I want to be near her.

Stupid, that impulse. It could lead nowhere but to trouble. Quint lowered his eyelids, smiled slowly.

Their eyes met.

She sucked in her breath.

He heard it all the way down the aisle.

Quickly, she turned, reached for the overhead bin. In this private jet the bins were more lavish than on commercial liners, but she struggle to get her suitcase stuffed in.

Quint hopped from his seat. In one long-legged stride, he was beside her. "Here, let me help with that."

For a second, she looked as if she might argue, but when he reached for the handle, she let go just as his fingers touched hers. He caught a whiff of her delicate perfume, and he was jonesing for something sweet.

"Thank you," she said, her soft voice as tender as a caress.

He was aware of a humming noise inside his brain, fraught with sexual energy. He stared at her lips, full and pink and shiny with gloss. His heart skipped another beat. What was the deal here? Was he developing a heart condition over Jorgie Gerard?

Frowning, Quint ripped his gaze from her distracting lips and fell into the pool of her deep blue eyes. He just stood there staring, her suitcase raised over his head, the bag braced against the cargo bin and his forearms.

Snap out of it.

"Is there a problem?" She lifted a hand to push back a tendril of hair from her face, the gold bracelets at her wrist jangling as they brushed against each other.

"Um..." *Do something, don't just stand there.*

The aisle was clogging up behind her. They were blocked the way. He shoved her suitcase into the overhead bin and clicked it closed.

"Thank you," she said, then sat down and snapped on her seat belt.

Not knowing what else to do, he mumbled, "You're welcome," and went back to his seat.

Still feeling a bit off balance, Quint settled into his seat and pried his mind from Jorgie and put it where it belonged.

On his job.

He was an air marshal on private security detail for the Lockhart Agency. For the last ten weeks, he and his fellow air marshals had been on assignment for Eros Airlines and Fantasy Adventure Vacations. The company's catchphrase was Something Sexy In The Air, and the business specialized in catering to a high-end clientele that enjoyed spending money indulging their sexual fantasies.

Over the course of the past several months, the airline's owner, Taylor Milton, had gotten anonymous threatening letters as someone had been sabotaging her four international resorts. She'd been reluctant to take her problems to the police and risk adverse publicity. To keep things discreet, she'd hired the Lockhart Agency to protect her interests.

The air marshals were undercover, both on the planes and at the resorts. Quint's undercover identity was an instructor at the Venetian facility, teaching a course on How To Make Love Like Casanova. It was silly to his way of thinking, but it was the most popular program Eros offered.

This was his third stint on the assignment and Quint had to admit he was having fun instructing students on how to be better lovers.

So far, the sabotages had been fairly minor, mere inconveniences than anything else. Until a month ago, when someone planted a small bomb at the Tokyo resort. The bomb had been found, the resort vacated, and the explosive neutralized with no harm done, but the situation had escalated. Taylor Milton had beefed up security at the resorts and ever since then, there'd been no more trouble and the threatening letters had stopped. It was eerie, waiting for the other shoe to drop.

Quint noticed no one took the seat beside Jorgie, but otherwise, the plane was full. Once they were airborne, he sent a text to his coworker Jake Stewart, who was at this very moment boarding a plane to Los Angeles for Eros's Make Love Like A Movie Star adventure.

He texted Jake. Everything looks normal here. U?

Jake: Same.

Quint: How'd your date go last night?

Jake: Don't ask. Jake had been divorced for over a year, and he'd finally started dating again.

Quint: That bad?

Jake: Door's closing. Later.

Shaking his head, Quint powered down his phone. The flight attendant was distributing drinks, and he heard Jorgie order a Bloody Mary. After she'd been served her drink, he took the bottle of water the attendant gave him and slipped into the seat beside Jorgie.

"Rough night?" he asked, wondering why he wanted so badly to talk to her.

She startled. "Huh?"

"Hair of the Dog?"

"Huh?"

He nodded at her drink. "A Bloody Mary is a common hangover cure."

"Oh." She shook her head. "No, in fact, I rarely drink..."

"Fear of flying?"

"Not at all."

"The mystery deepens." His nose twitched. She smelled so good. Like springtime flowers and maple syrup.

She straightened her shoulders, and a determined expression drifted over her face. "Drinking in the morning is new for me. I'm doing things I wouldn't normally do."

"Ah, bad breakup."

Her eyes widened. "How do you know that?"

"You're traveling alone, drinking a Bloody Mary, and headed to an Eros resort vacation. Common cure for a bad breakup."

"You're saying I'm a cliche?"

He shrugged and grinned. "Nothing wrong with that. We've all been there."

"I wasn't meant to be traveling alone. My friend Avery was supposed to come with me, but at the last minute she changed her ticket, hopped on a plane to another Eros resort, and left me holding the bag. I think I'm due a Bloody Mary, don't you?"

"For sure. I'll order you another." He lifted a finger at the flight attendant.

She looked at the water bottle in his hand. "You're not drinking?"

"Not in the mood, but you go right ahead." He widened his smile.

"That grin gets you laid a lot, doesn't it?"

Whoa, he hadn't expected such frank talk from the girl next door. "I do all right."

"Oh?" She lowered her lashes and slanted him a come-hither glance. "I'm all ears."

Heat burned its way up Quint's neck. Was she interested in him? He was certainly interested in her, but that was a big problem. He was on assignment. On the job. Fooling around with the guests was a no-no.

"I don't kiss and tell."

"Aah, the noble knight." She twirled a lock of hair and leaned in closer to him.

Not his imagination, she was definitely flirting with him. His heart skipped a beat, and he suddenly felt tongue-tied, which wasn't like him. He had to be careful. She was on the rebound and he was on the job.

Go back to your seat.

He did not. Instead, he studied Jorgie. "You've changed."

She arched her eyebrows. "And you haven't."

"What does that mean?"

"You still ooze charm from every pore."

"You think I'm charming?" He felt ridiculously pleased.

"I think you think you're charming."

Ouch, the kitten had claws. This was interesting. Quint leaned back and buckled his seat belt. He could do his job just as easily sitting here as in the last row.

"What are you doing?" she asked.

"Do you mind if I sit here? It's a long flight and we've got a lot of catching up to do."

"I suppose not."

"So tell me about the breakup."

"You're interested in the gory details of my sob story?"

"I am."

"Why?"

"Because you're fascinating."

"Seriously?" She rolled her eyes.

"I mean it. I'm intrigued." He didn't miss the quick grin that flashed across her face before it disappeared into narrowed eyes and a tilted chin notched up at him.

"Have you ever been engaged, Quint?"

"Not even close."

"Ever wanted to get married?"

"Never really crossed my mind."

She took a sip of her Bloody Mary and pointed a finger at him. "Smart man."

"This guy who dumped you, what was the matter with him?"

"He told me I was boring."

"Sounds like his problem, not yours."

She bit her bottom lip and looked away. "I *am* boring. That's why I'm headed to Venice. I need to shake things up."

"How's Keith?" he asked, not wanting to belabor her breakup with a guy who sounded like a total jerk. "We shot the breeze at or tenth high school reunion last year and we've exchanged a few emails since then, but we haven't been in touch lately."

"That's because Keith just got married, and he and his wife are expecting a baby girl in the fall. He's totally into fatherhood.

Quint felt disappointed that he hadn't been invited to the wedding. By why would he have been invited? He and Keith hadn't really kept in touch.

"Keith and Kylie eloped," Jorgie said, reading his mind. "No one was invited."

"Keith is married, huh. No kidding. But he's only..."

"Twenty-nine, the same age as you are. He's truly happy, and Kylie has been so good for him. He's going to be such a good dad."

"I'm thrilled for Keith. Truly." An odd wistfulness swept over him. It seemed all his buddies were getting married. He didn't get it. There was so much living to be done. A guy could get married and grow old anytime, but you were only young once.

"How's your parents?" she asked.

"They followed their bliss and moved to Santa Fe. Mom runs an art gallery. Dad takes tourists on guided hunts."

"And your brother?"

"Gordy's still in the Air Force. He's gonna be just like Dad. Career military."

"But not you?"

"Naw. I've never been much for having other people tell me what to do. The service wasn't a natural fit for me, but I did learn a lot while I was there."

"I wondered why you joined up. Structure doesn't seem like your strong suit."

"It was a struggle." He met her eyes and felt a hot zing of attraction. "But I'm more adaptable than you might imagine."

She dropped his gaze and settled her hands in her lap.

"How *are* your parents?" he asked.

"They sold their house on Janie Lane, moved into a condo in downtown Fort Worth."

"Wow that is a change."

"After years of suburban living, they wanted to be where the action was."

"I'm impressed. Paula and James living it up in Sundance Square, who knew?" He raked his gaze over her, and despite his best effort not to stare, couldn't stop himself from taking in the swell of her breasts beneath her blouse.

Knock it off, Mason.

"What are you up to these days?" he asked. "Keith told me you worked for a big accounting firm and that you'd gotten your CPA."

"I've been at the company since college. See, boring."

"Is it the only job you've ever had?"

"Other than working at Six Flags when I was a teen."

"Hey, Keith and I worked there the same summer. At the ice cream emporium."

"I remember. You got fired for giving free banana splits to pretty girls."

"That memory of yours..." Quint shook his head and grinned wide. "It's wicked dangerous."

Their gazes locked and that same compelling zap he'd felt when he bumped into her in the airport flashed through him again.

"Tell me, what is it you do?" she asked. "When you flattened me in the terminal, you said you were late for work. I thought you must be a pilot or flight attendant or something."

"I work for Eros," he said.

She eyed him. "In what capacity?"

"I'm an instructor at the resort," he lied, giving her his cover story, and it bothered him he had to fib to her.

"What do you teach?"

"The most popular course at the resort. How To Make Love Like Casanova."

Jorgie almost choked on her Bloody Mary. "You're serious?"

"Yep."

She giggled and polished off her drink.

"Hey, it's not *that* funny." He pretended to look hurt. Hell, if a guy couldn't laugh at himself, what could he laugh it? The Casanova thing *was* pretty goofy.

"You teach the art of seduction?"

He squirmed in his seat. "Something like that."

"Are you practicing your seduction skills on me now?" she asked.

"On an old friend?" He made a no-way face and shook his head. "I'm just enjoying our conversation."

"Really?"

"Scout's honor." He held up two fingers.

"Then how come you've got your elbow at the level of my breasts? Hoping for an accidental boob graze?"

"What? No!" He moved his arm. He hadn't intended that at all, but now that she'd brought it up, all he could think about were her breasts. He was so aware of her, and the air lay thick between them.

"Well," he said, "I better be getting back to my seat."

"Running away already?" She lowered her lashes.

"Yep."

"Why? We were just getting reacquainted."

"I'm in over my head with you, Little Bit."

Little Bit. His nickname for her when they were teens. Until now, he'd forgotten he used to call her that and he hoped she wasn't offended.

Her grin was loose, relaxed. "Bye then." She wriggled her fingers. "Parting is such sweet sorrow."

"I could stay…"

"Nah." She waved him away. "Absence makes the heart grow fonder."

"What about out of sight, out of mind?"

"Well…" She pursed those gorgeous pink lips. "There is that."

The last thing he wanted was to leave, but he was definitely in over his head. He had a powerful urge to lean over and kiss her silly.

"The guy's a dumbass," Quint said.

"What guy?"

"The one who broke up with you."

"That's sweet of you to say." The pain he saw in her eyes was a punch to the gut. He hated that she was hurting.

"I know it feels like your heart will never recover, but you're better off without him. You need someone who loves you and cherishes everything about you. You're gonna be okay, Jorgie. I promise."

Overwhelmed by his unexpected proclamation, Quint hopped up and hurried back to his seat, his mind reeling with the stunning realization that he wanted to be the one to mend her broken heart.

Chapter 3

Avery Bodel got off the plane in L.A. feeling freer than she'd felt in, well... forever.

She loved Jorgie like a sister, but the girl was so stuck in her ways. Sometimes it felt as if she was hanging out with an anchor. She did feel a bad for having ditched her friend at the airport the way she had, but it was for Jorgie's good. It was high time Jorgie started having adventures of her own without using Avery as a crutch.

Avery stood with the rest of the passengers at the private airstrip, waiting for her baggage to be unloaded from the Eros jet, when she saw *him* step off the plane.

He must have boarded earlier than she had and been sitting in the back of the plane, because she didn't remember ever seeing the guy before and he was not someone you could miss.

If this had been a Hollywood movie, this would be the point where the director cued the sensual music and softened the spotlight to focus on the drop-dead gorgeous man stepping off the plane.

Everything about him was dark. Dark hair, dark eyes, dark clothes, dark broody look on his face. Avery's heart thumped. Dude, now this was a M-A-N.

He wore faded black jeans with a hole in the right knee, a black Nirvana T-shirt that had been washed one too many times. He had on scuffed, scarred military boots and the beard stubble at his jaw declared that he hadn't seen a razor in days.

Dressed like this, some men might come across as scruffy and unkempt, but this guy sizzled like a downed power line.

Avery felt an instant stirring inside her and a longing for something more. Alarmed, she slapped the snooze button on her biological clock.

The last thing she wanted was anything—or anyone—tying her down. She couldn't be footloose with a diaper bag hanging off her shoulder and a kid on her hip. She was only twenty-five. She had a lot more living to do before she settled down.

As the oldest of five children, with her baby sister thirteen years younger, she knew all too well how kids consumed your life.

She gave herself a mental shake, but she couldn't stop staring at the guy. He possessed a keep-your-distance aura that made her itch to crowd his personal space.

He stepped from her line of sight, and it was only when she felt her shoulders sag that she realized how tense she'd been.

The attendants set suitcases on the tarmac, and everyone gathered around to claim their luggage. Avery and Mr. Broody Loner reached for the same black travel bag at the same time. She got there first, but his hand closed over hers.

His warm touch was firm and distracting.

Goose bumps spread up her arm.

"That's my bag," he said, his deep, evocative voice underscoring the authoritative expression on his face.

His rugged good looks created a masculine allure that could turn a vulnerable woman looking for a little excitement into a mindless pile of quivering flesh. Good thing she wasn't the quivery, vulnerable type.

"No." She stood her ground. "No, it's not. That's my bag."

"It's mine," he said. "And I can prove it."

Before she could react, he reached for the zipper and, in one smooth movement, unzipped the bag, just as she yanked on the handle. An array of brightly colored thong panties, push-up bras, racy negligees and sex toys spilled out onto the tarmac.

Instantly, his face bloomed red. "Um... um..."

"It's okay to admit your wrong, dude." Avery wrinkled her nose and tossed him a smug smile. If Jorgie were here, she'd be mortified. As it was, Avery was having a bit of fun.

"These..." He swept a hand at her sexy lingerie. "This is..."

"Mine," she said, not the least bit embarrassed to have the contents of her underwear drawer strewn around for everyone to see. She wasn't ashamed of her sexuality, and she didn't mind letting him know that. "And I do accept your apology, Mr...."

He laughed then, a rusty noise that sounded as if he didn't use it often. "Stewart," he said. "Jake Stewart."

She stuck out her hand. "Nice to meet you, Jake. I'm Avery, Avery Bodel."

He shook her hand with a steady grip and the sweet zap to her solar plexus turned her inside out. "Sorry about unzipping your bag. I could have sworn it was mine."

"Well, you'll just have to make it up to me." No one had ever accused Avery of being subtle.

"Sure, sure." He went down on one knee, started plowing through the plethora of panties, bras, teddies, and camisoles scattered over the ground. Red, black, white, green, purple. Silk, satin, lace.

She watched him, amused.

"You own stock in Victoria's Secret?" he asked.

"I should, considering all the money I spend in their stores."

With a thumb and forefinger, he picked up a vibrator, and then raised his head to meet her gaze, one eyebrow cocked.

"Don't judge." She snatched it from him. "A girl doesn't always have access to a fellow who's ready, willing, and able." She was charmed to see the tops of his ears bum beet-red. She'd rattled a guy who seemed unshakable.

"Hard to believe you have any trouble getting guys."

"Just because a woman can get a guy, it doesn't mean she wants him."

"Does anything embarrass you?" he asked.

"Not much."

He stuffed the last of her undergarments back in the bag and zipped it securely shut. "There you go."

"I've decided how you're going to make it up to me," she said.

"Huh?" He squinted at her.

"You need to pay a price for your snafu."

"How's that?"

"You're taking me out to dinner tonight." With that parting remark, she gathered up her bags and sashayed away.

———◉———

JAKE WATCHED HER GO, feeling as if he'd been caught in a tidal wave.

Avery Bodel was a force of nature, and he found her interesting as hell. It was in her sassy walk and her silky-smooth voice. He smelled her confidence in her scent—earthy, spicy, rich. He felt it on his skin where she'd shook his hand, pure energy, forceful and frightening. He saw it in the swing of her long dark purple hair and in that sassy little ink art peeking between the top of her low-rise jeans and the hem of her T-shirt.

The sight of that tattoo hardened his body and startled the hell out of him. He hadn't had such a powerful reaction to a woman in a long time. Not since Amanda. Not since before Afghanistan.

At the thought of the war, Jake grabbed up his bag filled with camera equipment and followed the rest of the group toward the waiting bus that would take them to the Eros resort nestled in the Hollywood Hills.

Normally, he didn't let himself get distracted, but a woman like Avery could make a man forget his own name.

And he didn't like it. Not one damned bit. He got the feeling she had only one speed, and that was balls to the wall. He wondered if she slowed down for anything.

The idea of finding out held far too much appeal. He wasn't about to take her out on a date. Miss Bodel was going to find herself disappointed if she thought she could just say the word and he'd fall right into line.

It appeared she was accustomed to wrapping men around her little finger, but she hadn't counted on Jake Stewart. Nobody told him what to do. Not anymore. Not since he'd left the Air Force the same time as his buddy Quint. Then a startling thought occurred to him.

What if Avery Bodel was the saboteur who'd been messing around with Taylor Milton's resorts?

Jake canted his head, watched her bounce as she mounted the steps to the bus. His boss, Dougal Lockhart, had told him to suspect everyone—guests, employees, even resort security. No one was above suspicion.

And Jake was adept at distrusting people, which was why he enjoyed viewing the world from behind a camera lens.

His talent at video photography was the reason Dougal and Taylor had decided his skills would be best suited to an undercover assignment at the Hollywood resort, making people's voyeuristic fantasies come true through film as he provided undercover scrutiny for Eros.

Could Avery Bodel be a saboteur?

Nah, unlikely. She didn't have a poker face. He'd seen the flare of sexual interest in her eyes, and he hadn't missed the goosebumps that flared up her arm when they'd touched.

He'd gotten goosebumps too.

His instincts told him that with this woman, what you saw was what you got. Then again, Samson never suspected Delilah and look what happened to him.

Forcing aside thoughts of the spunky Miss Bodel and her luscious body, Jake boarded the bus for the trip to the Eros resort.

He felt an itch to take the camera from the bag and start filming Avery, just so he could figure out what he thought about her. He splayed a palm to the back of his neck. *Stop thinking about her.* He had a job to do, and he let nothing impede his work. Not even a woman like Avery.

They arrived at the resort and got checked in. Jake enjoyed seeing the guests' reaction to the over-the-top glitz and glamour of the resort. It put him in mind of an R-rated version of the MGM Grand in Las Vegas. Lavish fountains, sexy movie posters, provocative music piped in through the sound system, clips of erotic scenes being played out on television monitors scattered throughout the resort. As guests checked in, the TV streamed 50 Shades of Grey.

He walked up to Avery, who stood in line for the registration desk. "Excuse me."

She turned to him. "Yes?"

"About that date—"

"Pick me up at eight," she said. "And take a razor to your chin. I'm not a fan of stubble burn."

As if he had planned to kiss her. Audacious woman. "Anyone ever tell you that you're bossy as hell?"

"All the time." She batted her lashes.

"Yeah, well, this dog doesn't jump when you snap your fingers. Sorry, I'm otherwise occupied. I can't make the date."

She didn't appear the least bit perturbed. "You're standing me up?"

"I am."

"I can see why you're not married."

"How do you know I'm not married?"

"For one thing, no ring. For another, I asked the bus driver."

"You asked about me?" Good God, why did that make him feel special?

"Of course. If we're going to be dating, I have to know you're not married. I don't date married men. I got burned once, never again."

"We're not dating."

She smiled at him as if he was a slow learner. '

"Next," called the desk clerk.

She maneuvered her luggage to the counter. Jake followed.

"We're not," he said.

"Uh-huh."

God, but the woman was irritating. He wouldn't stand here and argue with her. He'd already assigned a bungalow. He didn't have to wait in line. Shouldering his bag, he walked off and he could swear he heard her giggling behind him.

Amused, he headed for the back exit, wondering what it was about the woman that had gotten under his skin. He didn't enjoy feeling this way. Emotions were messy, troublesome things. He preferred to keep himself above the fray and now she had him squelching emotional impulses right and left.

He let himself into the bungalow decorated to replicate a 1940s era movie set and dumped his bag on the floor.

The table had a green Formica top that reminded him of the one that used to sit in his grandmother's kitchen and then he took his gun from the holster strapped to his leg and laid it beside the camera bag.

He made a quick call to check in with the Lockhart Agency. After that, he moved toward the bathroom. He wanted a cool shower after a long flight.

But he never made it to the shower.

He passed through the bedroom, and he noticed the blinds were open. He moved across the black-and-white tiled floor to draw them closed, and always the watcher, he peeked outside first.

Across the way, in the next bungalow, the blinds were open, as well. The distance between the two dwellings wasn't more than three feet, and he could see right inside the other bedroom.

What he saw froze him to the spot with his hand wrapped around the swivel rod of the blinds. His shaft hardened, rising to strain against the zipper of his jeans.

In the bedroom next door, Avery Bodel was stripping off her clothes right in front of the open window. Her back was to him as she pulled her shirt over her head and tossed it to the floor. Her hands went to the clasp of her bra, and she undid each eye hook. He could see the ink art on her lower back, a simple dark blue design of tangled vines.

As he watched her, his throat tightened.

She slipped off the bra and turned, giving him a side view of her perfect breasts. Not too big, not too small, just the right size in his estimation. She unsnapped her jeans and shimmied them over her hips, leaving her standing there in nothing but a spectacular red satin thong.

His erection throbbed. He should snap the blinds closed or step away from the window, but he couldn't make himself move. Nothing could wrench his gaze from the glory of her feminine curves.

She reached up to pull her hair into a ponytail and secure it high on her head with a band. Her complexion was flawless, but he grinned when he spied the cute little dimple in the center of her right butt cheek.

Jake gulped. Turn away. Turn away.

But he did not. Could not.

She lifted one long, lean leg up to the comer of the bed, leaned over to peel off her sock, and then repeated it with her other leg.

His breath was coming in hot, raspy gasps. All the muscles in his body tensed. A groan slipped from his lips and his fingers tightened as he imagined sinking them into the sweet flesh of her rounded bottom and holding on for dear life as he pumped into her.

With her back still to him, she hooked her index finger through the tiny little scrap that made up her panties and inched the material down, wriggling her hips.

His erection was blindingly hard. He couldn't even think, much less breathe. Sweat beaded his forehead.

Then she turned, head down, as she kicked off her panties, giving him a full and unobstructed view of her body. Those perfect breasts sported pert pink nipples. A golden ring glinted at her navel. That sweet patch of hair just above her sex told him she was a natural blonde through and through.

She raised her head, stared right into his bedroom window, and slyly winked just before she reached out and shuttered the blinds.

Chapter 4

Venice was an architectural symphony. A simmering fantasy of mist and sunshine, a meandering labyrinth of pathways, bridges and canals and a sweet poem of complex dreams.

Jorgie had often daydreamed of visiting the most romantic city on earth. She'd visualized herself strolling the cobblestone streets, gliding the waterways in a graceful gondola, shopping in the popular Rialto district. She imagined she would stop to watch artisans expertly practice the art of blowing glass or mask-making. She'd thirsted to drink Bellinis at a sidewalk cafe.

And she'd ached to kiss Brian on the Bridge of Sighs.

So much for the last part, but she didn't require a man to enjoy Venice. She was on her own in a foreign country and it felt thrilling. Avery had been right. She needed to go it alone for once.

Their group arrived via vaporetto, a water taxi sardined with Eros guests, and by the time they reached the resort, Jorgie was in love. How had she lived twenty-five years without Venice?

Smiling hosts, costumed in period clothing from the Italian Renaissance, greeted the guests at the lavish resort, a restored Venetian palace once occupied by royalty. She searched for Quint in the crowd but didn't see him, and the bite of disappointment was unexpected.

She checked in and turned to go to her room when she spied him, and her heart went all wonky again.

He was dressed like an eighteenth-century nobleman, in rich fabrics and lush colors of the time. He seemed taller than he'd been on the plane, his eyes sharper, his presence regal. His large personality and jovial laugh filled the room as he said something to the dozen women who'd collected around him.

Casanova in the flesh.

He glanced over the heads of the other women, caught her gaze, and offered a lopsided smile meant only for her.

The other women gaped at him with dumbstruck expressions, as if the heavens had opened up and he'd come tripping down the stairs just for them. They hung on to his every word. Groupies.

Who knew he had groupies?

Although she longed to join the flock, something inside of Jorgie would not let her puddle at his feet.

Yes, he was handsome. Yes, his smile stirred her soul. Yes, she'd had a crush on him when she was thirteen. Yes, she wanted to kiss him so badly she couldn't breathe, but she wouldn't let Quint know. And be like all the others? No way. She had her pride.

She turned, headed toward the exit.

"Jorgie," he called.

Well, she couldn't very well ignore him now, could she? That would be rude. She stopped, turned back.

"Quint, oh, hi, I wasn't sure that was you." Great, now she was lying.

"Excuse me, ladies." He threw the women a lazy grin, and they seemed to melt to the spot. "I need to speak to an old friend."

He covered the distance with long-legged strides, and when he linked his arm through Jorgie's she lost her breath.

Laughing, he pulled her into an alcove. "Thanks, Little Bit."

"I can't believe you remembered that you and Keith used to call me that," she said, feeling way more flattered than she should. He'd called her Little Bit as a big brotherly term of affection, and it meant he viewed her as a little sister or an old friend, not as a potential lover.

"Well..." He raked his gaze over her. "I shouldn't use the nickname on you. It's Little Bit no more. You're all grown up."

"What were you thanking me for?" she asked, glossing right over that.

He punched the button for the elevator. "Rescuing me from my adoring public."

Jorgie snorted. "Hey, if you can't handle the adoration, don't dress up like Casanova."

"You do not know what a huge burden it is..." Laughing, he struck a preening pose. "Being such a sexy beast."

Jorgie rolled her eyes. "Poor you."

"You're pitiless."

"I have little tolerance for nonsense—"

"You're good for me," he said. "I need someone to call me on my ego. I gotta admit, playing Casanova messes with my head."

"Don't blame Casanova. You were like that in high school, and I have a feeling you've been like that ever since."

He looked into her eyes. "You overestimate me. I'm not the playboy this costume makes me out to be."

"Uh-huh," she said, not buying it for a second.

"What room are you in?" he asked as the elevator opened and he got on with her.

She should have told him it was none of his business, but damn if that endearing grin of his didn't slip past her defenses. "214."

"The blue room." He punched the elevator button for the second floor. "Madame de Pompadour stayed there. Did you know she and Casanova were lovers?"

"Who is Madame de Pompadour?"

"A wealthy patron of the arts."

"So she mixed business with pleasure. Not a smart move."

"My guess is she wasn't so sensible about it." He studied her as the elevator moved upward. "Unlike you. You're more like Lady Evangeline."

"Who is that?"

"You'll find out."

"Trying to intrigue me?"

"Is it working?"

"Marginally," she said.

Jake laughed. The elevator settled on the second floor with a ping, and they got off together.

"You're mocking me."

He lowered his eyelids and slanted a sexy look her way. "It's hard not to. You look so serious."

They walked down the corridor; the plush carpeting cushioning their steps. "Here we are," she said. "214. You've escorted me to my room. You can go now."

Jorgie tapped the key card against the card reader on the door handle, it clicked, and she kneed the door open.

"Wait." He touched her forearm.

Instantly, the hairs on her arms lifted, and her heart vaulted into her throat. He said nothing for a moment. His gaze hooked on her. She forced herself to hold his stare.

"Yes?"

"Sit with me at dinner."

"Why?"

"Fend off the she wolves?"

"Don't give me that. You love the she wolves."

"Okay, here's the deal. You remind me of home. I don't see my folks much. Gordy's married with kids. I just wanted someone to talk to." He sounded sincere.

But Jorgie didn't trust it. She narrowed her eyes. "This isn't some Casanova ploy to get me into bed, is it?"

"I'm shocked that you would suggest such a thing." He feigned innocence. "Is it working?"

Yes. "No."

"Come on." His cajoling gaze caressing her face. "Dinner? For old times' sake?"

A shiver of awareness tripped down Jorgie's spine, dueling madly with the part of her that wanted to invite him to join her in bed. She couldn't stop the gut-level reaction that whispered, go for it.

The problem was that pesky junior high crush. If he was just a good-looking guy interested in a fun time, she might take a walk on the wild side. He could easily be her first ever casual fling. But there was that nagging infatuation that had had her doodling in her notebook, *Mrs. Jorgie Mason.*

She had two fears. One, what if she had a fling with Quint and it turned out to be lousy?

The sweet fantasy of him would be lost to her forever. Then there was the very real possibility that sex with him would be dynamic, unlike anything she'd ever experienced, and she'd fall in love with him all over again, while he blithely went on his merry way. She wasn't in any emotional condition to deal with that.

He flashed her one of his trademark smiles, and for a fraction of a second, that devilish come- play-with-me grin had her on the edge of throwing caution to the wind. Then she thought about how he'd given her that same smile when he was sixteen just before he pulled a prank on her.

Still...

He was right. They would both be eating dinner in the main dining hall with the tour group. Why not sit at his table? He'd once been her brother's best friend. It would be rude, wouldn't it, to deny his request? Plus, they'd be in a public place. What could happen?

"All right," she said, although she didn't know why. The cold shoulder she'd given him on the plane was really the only way to deal with a charming guy like Quint, especially when she was feeling so vulnerable.

"See you at eight." He winked and strolled out the door.

Jorgie stared after him, awash in the wake of his sexiness. What in the devil had she just opened herself up for?

She'd gotten what she'd come on this trip for, a date with a hot guy to help her forget about Brian. But she hadn't expected that man to be the same guy who'd once dominated her girlhood fantasies.

A guy who made her feel both shivery and sweaty at the same time.

This was her chance for a true, no-strings sexual adventure. She should grab it with both hands and hang on for dear life.

———————●———————

AN HOUR LATER, QUINT was sitting in a plush leather chair in an equally plush office that made him antsy. He'd been summoned by Taylor Milton herself, who'd just flown in on her private jet, and he couldn't help wondering what he'd done wrong.

Taylor was thirty-four and looked exactly like what she was, an airline heiress. Five foot six, red-haired and sharp-eyed, a lithe package of ballerina grace and bulldog tenacity that had shot her to the top of an industry that had fallen on challenging times.

She'd taken her father's plain vanilla commuter airline and turned it into the only adult-oriented airline/destination resort in the world. She was a fair boss but demanding. She wanted what she wanted whenever she wanted it. Nor was she a woman easily swayed by an easy grin.

On that score, she reminded him of Jorgie.

As he sat there, his anxiety growing, his boss, Dougal Lockhart, walked through the door.

Uh-oh. The shit must have hit the fan if they were tag-teaming him.

Quickly, Quint considered what might have triggered this meeting. The morality clause he'd signed for Eros forbade him from having sex with the guests, but it didn't say a word about fellow employees.

On his last tour here, he and Gwen, the woman who'd played the part of his Casanova conquest for the stage play, had had a very good time together. Was that what this was about? Had he crossed a line? The last thing he ever wanted was to make any woman feel uncomfortable around him. He did enjoy himself, but never at someone else's expense.

Dougal stalked over and perched on the corner of Taylor's desk.

"What's up?" Quint flashed his ready smile.

"Taylor's received another threatening letter," Dougal said. "And we've determined it was written on a computer at this resort. Unfortunately, it was from a computer in the internet cafe, so anyone could have sent it."

"There's a log-in record," Quint said.

"Yes, but if someone leaves without signing out, anyone can take their place and still be logged in under the first person's name," Taylor said. "In fact, we suspect the perpetrator haunted the cafe just waiting for someone who forgot to log out."

Quint got feeling someone had sent the e-mail under his name. He wracked his brain trying to think of the last time he'd used the internet cafe. "Who did you trace it back to?"

"Gwen Kemp," Dougal said.

Quint winced. "You think Gwen is in on the sabotage?"

Taylor shifted in her seat, picked up a pencil and drummed it against the top of her desk. "We don't believe so. Dougal grilled her for over an hour and she does have airtight alibis for most of the sabotage incidents that have occurred at the resorts over the course of the last several months."

"I'm sensing a 'but' here," Quint said.

"But we can't take any chances, so Gwen has been suspended until we can determine who sent the e-mail under her address."

"You might never find out."

"We'll find out," Dougal said. "This crap stops now."

"I agree. You got a copy of the e-mail?"

Dougal pulled a folded printout from his pocket and passed it to Quint.

He unfolded it and read the vitriolic message.

No more pussyfooting around, Princess, this is it. You're going down in a big way. After I get through with you, you'll be standing in line for food stamps. You think those air marshals you hired as security for your planes and resorts can protect you? They have done little good so far. I'll hit when and where you least expect it. Nothing will stop me. Ciao for now.

"This is personal," Quint looked up from the printout to meet Taylor's gaze.

Dougal nodded solemnly. "We need to be hypervigilant."

"Of course."

"There's also the matter of Gwen's replacement," Taylor said. "We don't have time to hire and train another actress to play the part of your love conquest for the course."

"You're ditching the class." Quint sat up straighter in his chair. He wouldn't mind ditching the Casanova costume.

"No," Taylor said. "We have thirty-seven men signed up for your course. Enrollment has skyrocketed since you took over the class."

"I told you he was a natural-born charmer," Dougal said.

"He's hot." Taylor nodded. "You have that nice blend of boyish charm and flirtatious audacity that people go gaga over. If you weren't working for Dougal, I'd hire you in a heartbeat."

Quint felt a twin surge of pride and a tinge of embarrassment. Truth was, he enjoyed playing Casanova, but he was also sheepish about it. He shrugged. "Aw, shucks, ma'am, it's nothing."

"See, right there." Taylor pointed. "That's what I'm talking about. You know you're handsome, but you have a way about you that says you don't take it too seriously."

"Life's too short to take it seriously."

"Exactly."

"So if you're not replacing Gwen with a new actress and you're not canceling the course, who will Casanova seduce?"

"Me," Taylor said.

Quint gulped. The woman scared him. "You?"

"I'm happily married," Taylor said. "I'm immune."

"Maybe," Quint said, "but Casanova's romance is going to look like the put-up job it is if anyone recognizes you."

"Do you have a better idea?" Dougal asked.

He thought of Jorgie. "I do."

Taylor leaned back in her chair. "I'm all ears."

"An old friend of mine is staying at the resort," Quint said. "I've known her since we were teenagers. We're just friends, and she's here nursing a broken heart. I think she'd be the perfect person to play Casanova's conquest."

"Hmm." Taylor studied him pensively. "It's a thought."

"Do you think she'll agree to do it?" Dougal asked.

"I'm having dinner with her tonight. I'll ask," he said, searching for anything to keep from having Taylor play Madame de Pompadour.

"I don't know," Taylor mused. "Could this cause trouble in your relationship with her?"

"Don't worry," Quint said. "She really is just a friend." Although she had grown up to be a beauty.

"Well, then." Taylor beamed. "Ask her. If she can't do it, I'm the fallback plan."

Dougal called the head of resort security, Frank Lavoy, a barrel-chested man in his mid-forties who'd worked under Dougal when they were in the air force together, into the office for the rest of the meeting. Dougal launched into the heightened security protocol they'd instituting at all the resorts and his expectations from Quint and Frank.

Quint listened, nodded, absorbed the information, but in the back of his mind, his thoughts were on Jorgie. He saw one major flaw in his plan.

One huge obstacle loomed. He'd flat-out lied to Taylor. He'd suddenly developed budding feelings for the woman who'd been his best friend's little sister.

A knock sounded on the door.

"Come in," Taylor said.

The door opened and an older, heavyset man with gray hair stepped over the threshold, a well-dressed woman in her early sixties by his side.

"Hey there, princess," the man said.

"Chuck, Mitzi." Taylor's face dissolved into a welcoming grin. She hopped from behind the desk and went to hug the couple. "What are you doing here?"

"We were in Rome," Mitzi said, "and Chuck remembered it was your birthday, so we called your office, and your secretary told us you were here, so of course we had to come to Venice. We haven't seen you since the wedding! How's Daniel?"

"Fabulous," Taylor said, referring to her new husband.

"We're taking you out to dinner," Chuck said. "And we won't take no for an answer."

"Dougal, Quint." Taylor gestured. "This is General Charles Miller and his wife, Mitzi. Dear friends of the family."

Quint and Dougal shook first General Miller's hand and then his wife's.

"Chuck and Mitzi are my godparents. They're the aunt and uncle I never had," Taylor said.

"Any leads on who could make those awful threats?" Mitzi asked.

Taylor sighed. "Not so far."

General Miller glowered. "Have you considered changing the direction of your resorts?"

"Meaning what?" Taylor asked.

The general shrugged. "Perhaps this person or persons would back off if your resorts weren't so..." He paused, choosing his words carefully. "Controversial."

Taylor sank her hands on her hips. "Are you suggesting I allow someone to threaten me into abandoning the business model that's made me so successful?"

"It might have made you successful—" Miller stiffened, and his eyes narrowed "—but it's also made you a target. If your father was alive—"

"My father would be amazed that I've tripled the net worth of his airline in six short years." Taylor frowned. "I know you don't approve of the concept of Eros resorts. Chuck, but I believe I provide a much-needed service, which my profits bear out."

"My," Mitzi said, clearly trying to change the topic, and she cast her gaze over Quint. "Don't you look dashing."

"Quint plays Casanova for our most popular course," Taylor said.

General Miller's face darkened. "The famous libertine?"

"It's just a costume," Quint said. "Some role-playing fantasies for the guests."

The general glowered, reminding Quint why he left the Air Force. Too much hierarchy and discipline for his tastes.

"Well, I don't know about you, Taylor," Mitzi said, "but I'm starving." She looked at her husband. "I made reservations for six-thirty and it's after six. Maybe we should go?"

"I'm ready." Taylor linked her arm through the general's, and she and Mitzi escorted him out the door.

Leaving Quint feeling vaguely uneasy about the general and his wife and no real reason for it.

Chapter 5

At seven-thirty, Jorgie put the finishing touches on her makeup in the bathroom of her courtesan-inspired bedroom suite. She walked into the lavish sitting area done up in rich fabrics, heavy furniture, and lushly detailed tapestries.

She could appreciate how Venetian courtesans had thrived in such sensual surrounds. The thick textures compelled the fingertips and velvet cushions stretched over smooth, hard mahogany chairs and adorned intricately woven brocade pillows. Shimmering golden threads sewn through burgundy damask, but the sensory appeal of the room did not stop with the tactile.

The room smelled of love as well. Real flowers adorned many vases, roses and stargazer lilies, and baby's breath scented the room with the sweet aroma of courtship. Their tender buds were like secret sex organs, releasing their aromatic juices into the air.

Heady stuff.

Jorgie, feeling unnerved and overwhelmed, retrieved her cell phone from her purse and then sank down on the couch that hugged her in an opulent embrace, and called Avery.

Her friend answered right away. "Hello?"

"Hey, you," Jorgie said.

"What's up?" Avery yawned.

Jorgie pushed a strand of errant hair back off her forehead. "I've got a date."

"Already?" Her friend's tone changed, and she could almost hear Avery's grin. "Wow, I should have abandoned you to your own devices a long time ago. So tell me about the guy?"

Jorgie hesitated, not sure she wanted to be completely honest with Avery. She worried she'd tease her, and she didn't want to be teased about Quint.

"Well? You *did* call me."

Jorgie cleared her throat. "It's Quint."

"Oooh, the plot thickens."

An emotion she couldn't name tap-danced around in her head. Jorgie bit down on her index finger. "I'm scared."

"Why?"

"I like him."

"And?"

"That's it. I like him."

"Why does that frighten you?"

"Because I know what he is and I know what kind of woman I am and, well... we don't match."

"Hey, this week isn't supposed to be a forever kind of love. This vacation is about exploring sexual horizons, and who better than a man you know and trust. He's perfect."

Sex with Quint. The image popped too readily into her mind. His hard body pressed against her soft one. It wasn't the first time she'd imagined such a fantasy. Not by a long shot.

"I know, and that's what scares me. I don't know if I *can* have a casual fling."

"Then don't have sex with him."

Alarm snapped through her as quick as whiplash. "But I want to."

"Then do it."

"I don't want to get hurt."

Avery sighed. "You think too much. Just go with the flow. Let it be. Let whatever happens be okay. Insert your carefree adage here. You can do this."

How very Zen.

Maybe thinking about numbers would help. Numbers calmed her. They were rational, expected, no surprise with numbers. No emotions, either. She took a deep breath. "Thanks for talking me down."

"No problem."

"So, how are things in L.A.?"

"Hmm," Avery said, "they're a bit frustrating."

"How so?"

"I spied a guy I was interested in on the plane. In fact, he's a cameraman for Eros. I asked him out for dinner, but he told me he wasn't interested."

"And you took no for an answer?"

"Well, for now."

"He won't know what hit him." Jorgie chuckled. "I'll let you go. Be safe."

"You, too."

She switched off her phone. A knock sounded on her door. She peered out the peephole and her stomach did a slow slide to her shoes.

Quint.

Looking exceedingly handsome in a suit and tie. How come he was picking her up? They were just supposed to meet in the dining hall. And why was he wearing a suit. Feeling self-conscious that she hadn't dressed up enough, Jorgie ran a hand over the front of her simple cotton sundress, dithering about whether to go change or not.

He knocked again.

Don't just stand there with your mouth open, let the man in.

Taking a deep breath to steady her jangled nerves, she opened the door.

Quint met her with a grin and his patented come-hither gaze, his dark hair combed back off his forehead. He smelled of soap and crisp green apples. The minute he saw her, his eyes flashed hot. He raked his eyes over her dress.

"Wow, you look great in green."

"Is it okay? I didn't realize dinner was so dressy, I mean, you're in a suit and—"

"You're perfect," he said, and extended his elbow to her. "Ready to go down to dinner?"

"Um... yes, you didn't have to come fetch me, you know."

"I know, but I wanted to. Is that okay?"

"Yes, sure, fine."

"Shall we?"

Not knowing what else to do, she linked her arm around his elbow.

They went downstairs to the elegant dining room. The buffet spread out before them was a feast for an entire kingdom. Prime rib and roasted chicken and braised pork tenderloin, vegetables of every variety served as delicious side dishes. There was rye bread and pumpernickel and thick yeasty loaves of French bread.

Jorgie loaded up her plate and followed Quint to a small bistro table for two. Most of the other guests were sitting at the long communal table.

"We can sit over there with everyone else," she said, nervous to be alone with him.

"I'd rather sit here." He set down his plate and gave her an encouraging smile. "There's something I want to discuss with you."

Oh, wow. What could that be? Blowing out her breath, she sat, and he took the seat across from her.

A moment of awkward silence stretched between them, and she zeroed in on his handsome face. He'd been cute as a teenager, but now he was stunningly handsome. Those full lips, that proud nose, those dark, enigmatic eyes.

She gulped.

He cleared his throat.

She smiled and then quickly ducked her head as she unfurled the black linen napkin over her lap. "What did you want to ask me?"

"I'm appealing to your sense of adventure."

Her head shot up, and she met his steady gaze. His dimpled grin shot pure electricity straight to her solar plexus.

"Y-yes?"

"I'd like you to be my conquest."

"Wh-what?" Heat flooded her body. Good grief, why was she stammering? "You mean you want to have sex with me?"

"No!" He stared at her. "Well, yes, but it's not what you think."

All the air left her lungs. "Wh-what is it?"

"Cards on the table?"

She nodded.

"I like you. I've always liked you. Seeing you again..." He paused.

Jorgie felt her eyes widen. She crossed her fingers in her lap. What was Quint about to propose? Hung on hope and anticipation, she waited, breath held.

"Well..." Both his eyes and his smile softened. "You feel safe. Like home."

Uh-oh. That sounded like friend zone territory. She exhaled. Disappointment tugged her heart to her stomach. Just to have something to do with her hands during this odd conversation, Jorgie picked up the steak knife. She held it with her thumb against the back of the blade.

"What I mean is," Quint said. "I trust you."

Her hopes chugged upward again. Still, she was uncertain what he was getting at. Did he want to have a fling with her? She certainly wanted one with him.

Please, let that be what he wanted.

"I feel like I started this conversation in the wrong place. Let me begin again." Quint placed both palms on the table. "My role here at Eros is to embody Casanova, and I need a conquest."

"Um, okay." She cut a neat slice of the chicken breast filet on her plate, took a bite and chewed thoughtfully, trying to camouflage her emotions. The sauce was quite delicious. A balsamic reduction.

"The woman who plays the role of my conquest had to leave the resort unexpectedly, so I'm without a partner to seduce as part of the show. If I don't have a partner, they'll have to cancel the class."

Ahh, he wasn't asking her to be his fling. He wanted her to be part of his course and pretend to be his lover.

Her feelings took a hit, just as they had in college when a cute guy she'd been mooning over asked her out and then in the middle of the date he'd tried to hire her to do his calculus homework. Same deal here. Same sour-stomach sensation and she felt stupid for thinking Quint had wanted her.

"There's no one else?" she asked, watching cut up his food in bite-sized pieces.

"Gwen just left this morning," Quint said. "But by the time they could hire someone, it would be too late for this course. So I was wondering, since we're friends, if you could help me out of this fix. If the resort cancels the course, I don't get paid."

She pondered that too as they ate in silence for a few minutes. Quint watched her, his dark-eyed gaze locked on her.

"What would I have to do?" she asked.

"Pretend to fall in love with me."

Yikes! That sounded dangerous. Like she could get hurt.

"What do I get out of the deal?" She took a sip of her drink.

"I've already talked to my boss about you replacing Gwen. Your trip to Eros would be comped."

Well, that was a deal. An Eros vacation did not come cheap.

Jorgie put down her silverware and raised a palm. "Let me get this straight. You want me to pretend to fall in love with you in front of the guys to whom you're teaching pickup artist techniques, and for that I get a free vacation?"

"That it."

Good thing she was sitting down because her knees wobbled, and her skin warmed like melted butter.

Quint pointed his fork at her. "But you can't make the conquest easy for me."

She cocked her head. "No? Why not? I thought that was Casanova's schtick. He had women falling at his feet."

"It has to look convincing. I need to show Casanova's seduction techniques. Besides, Casanova loved a challenge."

"Are we talking about Casanova here, or you?"

He looked sheepish. "Don't most men love the thrill of the chase?"

Jorgie studied him. He was speaking her language. She'd come to Eros to have the sexual adventure, and now he was offering it on a gilded platter.

"Let's say I agree. What would I have to do?"

"Play hard to get. Remember, the whole resort experience is part of the show. Right here, right now, I'm playing the part of Casanova."

She moistened her lip. "I think I get it. This whole date isn't between Quint and Jorgie. You're not you and I'm not me. You're Casanova and I'm your potential conquest."

"Yes, exactly."

Disappointment knocked down her spine, one bone at a time. None of this was real. It was all pretend. All part of the show.

"So right this very minute, we're on this date and you're trying to seduce me, as Casanova."

"Yes. We're setting the stage for my first class tomorrow morning."

"I see." She flicked out her tongue to moisten her lips and noticed his gaze locked on her mouth.

As Quint? Or Casanova?

Oh, this would be easier if she'd never had a schoolgirl crush on him. She weighed her options of getting the vacation for free versus the danger of losing her heart to Quint during this masquerade.

And made a swift decision.

"All right," she said. "I'll do it."

"Really?" The happy surprise on his face convinced her she'd made the right choice.

Seriously, what's the worst that could happen? A few passionate kisses from Quint as a souvenir of her time in Venice.

Sign me up!

"Are you up for starting now?" He glanced around. "Since we are in a public space and people are watching."

"Sort of set the tone for what's coming?"

"You got it." His dimples deepened.

"Sure." The idea was growing on her. This could be fun!

He leaned across the table and got so close to her ear she could feel his minty breath warm her cheek. "Act as if I said something morally repugnant."

"Huh?"

"Jump to your feet, knock over your chair, call me a name, slap me across the face."

Jorgie pulled back, shocked but also exhilarated. "I can't slap you."

"Why not?"

"You're Quint. My brother's best friend from high school. Besides, I don't hit people."

"You're not Jorgie. You're a famous courtesan. Believe me, she enjoyed slapping roguish Casanova."

"Did your previous partner put on such a show with you?"

"How do you think I know it's effective?"

The thought of doing what he asked and drawing undue attention to herself made Jorgie's stomach contract. "It sounds hinky."

"You don't have to smack me hard, just cause a scene."

"I'm not... This doesn't..." She hesitated. She didn't want to slap Quint. What she wanted was to kiss him. Her cheeks flushed hot at the thought.

"You're embarrassed."

"Yeah, well, sort of."

What he did next took her by surprise. One minute he was grinning at her impishly, the next minute he'd pulled her across the table and was full-on kissing her. Giving her what she wanted.

Both shock and delight shot through her. Not just from his kiss, but how damn quickly it aroused her. Startled, she jumped to her feet.

"That's it," he said. "Let me have it for boorishly manhandling you."

"How dare you!" She projected her voice as loudly as she could.

Heads turned. Conversations ground to a dead halt, and the fact that people were staring at her caused Jorgie's cheeks to bum.

"Good, good. You've got the hang of it."

"I've never been so insulted in my life!" When with that pronouncement, she slapped him lightly across the face, purposefully knocking over a chair as she stormed away.

The room fell dead silent.

Now she knew what it felt like to be a woodland creature crossing the road in the middle of the night just as a sports car zoomed around the corner.

Roadkill.

Chapter 6

Two hours later, Jorgie lay in bed staring at the ceiling, her body tingling from head to toe.

Embarrassed, Jorgie pulled a pillow over her face.

She couldn't stop remembering how it had felt to have Quint's firm lips pressed against hers, tantalizing, exciting, awe-inspiring. He hadn't meant it. She knew that, and she had to stop fantasizing about him.

She knew the kiss was all for show. How brief it had been. A second only. Two at the most and yet...

Whew!

She'd wanted more. So much damned more it freaked her out. *It was the unexpectedness of it.* There was nothing inherently terrific about his kiss.

Oh, you are such a liar.

She touched her nose to see if it was growing. Okay, fine. The kiss had been so spectacular she'd stopped breathing. What she'd secretly wanted, wished for, was for him to press harder and take the kiss deeper.

But not there in front of everyone, of course. Then again, if they'd been somewhere private, no telling how far he might have taken things. She blushed in the darkness, shamed by both her unexpected need and the silly theatrics she'd performed in the dining hall.

She needed some fun, to take Avery's advice and let whatever happens be okay.

That was difficult to do because while he'd kissed her, she'd known it was all for show. He meant nothing by it. He'd chosen her for his charade because she was safe—a pal, a friend, a buddy.

She clenched the sheets in her fists and let out a noise of frustration. Why had she agreed to this?

Free vacation.

Oh, yeah. But in retrospect, was it really worth it? Gnawing her bottom lip, she flipped over onto her side. *Sleep, sleep, go to sleep.*

She flopped onto her back again. This was a bad idea. She should simply tell Quint the deal was off. She didn't want to be his fake conquest.

She wanted to be his real one.

⎯⎯◉⎯⎯

"GIACOMO CASANOVA WAS born in Venice in 1725," Quint said to the group of men gathered for his class.

Many of his students were socially awkward types who lacked self-esteem when approaching women. Quint was confident that if they took his advice, they'd soon be on their way to exciting love lives, and he'd told them as much.

They'd sat up straighter just hearing that. Now they waited, eyes on him, poised to take notes.

He felt a thrill in teaching that he hadn't expected when he took the undercover assignment. He loved being an air marshal—the travel, the freedom, the excitement—but teaching filled a space in him he hadn't known was empty. Being an air marshal was about looking for the bad in people, but it was the nature of a teacher to find and nurture the good.

And Quint searched for the bright side, but no matter how much he was enjoying this avocation, he couldn't forget the real reason he was here.

To protect Taylor Milton and Eros Airlines.

He looked at his class roster and noticed the checkmarks beside three names, showing the men had taken the class before under the regular instructor, who'd been given a paid sabbatical while Quint assumed the faculty role. He would keep an extra-close eye on those students. They could be saboteurs.

"Casanova was the son of actors, which back then was considered an ignoble profession. Actors often made ends meet as prostitutes or pimps. As you might imagine, the young Casanova was deeply affected but his parents' professions."

The students took copious notes as Quint had their rapt attention.

"His parents traveled from town to town, plying their trade, and Casanova felt shame about his mother's reputation, but what hurt him most was her abandonment. He wrote in his memoirs about being sent away to Padua, where he received a formal education, but he was still bitter about being separated from her."

A hand in the back of the room shot up.

"Yes?" Quint pointed at the student.

"You expect us to believe that Casanova's kinky sexual behavior was his parents' fault?" a guy named Joe Vincent asked.

In every class there was always one—the smartass, the rebel, the contrarian who questioned everything. Also, Joe Vincent had taken the class last winter about the same time the Venetian resort was the first property to experience sabotage.

"Not at all, Joe," Quint said. "I'm just giving you a bit of background on what molded Casanova. We're all responsible for our own behavior."

"So what about you?" Joe asked. "How come you're not married if you're so good at seduction?"

"We're not talking about me."

"You're playing the part of Casanova," Joe said. "What motivates you? Mommy issues?"

The rest of the students snickered and glanced from Joe to Quint and back again. He had to take control of the class or things could turn ugly.

"Let's just say I haven't found the right woman yet."

"So you're not like Casanova, constantly in pursuit of happiness just beyond your grasp?"

Was he? The question blindsided him, but he pushed it aside and trudged on. "No."

Quint waited, fists curled at his sides, ready to defend his position. To his relief, Joe seemed to have lost interest in challenging him and shut up.

"Casanova was a complicated guy." Quint offered a ready smile at the group. "He received a doctor-of-law degree in Padua, proving his lifelong contention that the mind is the ultimate aphrodisiac."

"I like dirty talk." A guy called Raoul chortled.

Quint let that slide right on by. "Casanova used expressive language, among other tools and techniques, to seduce women, and that's part of what we'll learning during this two-week course. I'll also choose a woman from the resort guests to use Casanova's techniques on."

"You're going to seduce someone as a demonstration?" said a thin guy in his early twenties with thick-framed glasses and mussed-up hair named Troy. "Sweet!"

"Isn't that underhanded?" Raoul asked. "Toying with a woman's emotions?"

"Not in this context," Quint said, even though he felt uneasy about the whole thing. "All Eros guests sign an informed consent paperwork, just as you all did when they embark on these fantasy vacations."

"Well, if that's the case, how can we know your techniques actually work in the real world where people aren't primed for seduction?" Joe asked.

"I suppose only you can be the judge of that," Quint said. "But Casanova's reputation stands as a testament."

"Seriously, dude, what's your problem?" Troy asked. "Why are you being a pain in the ass? We're here because we want to be like Casanova."

Conflicted, Quint paused. This was a moral gray. While everyone at the resort was consenting adult, looking for a fantasy experience, he couldn't help wondering if he was contributing to a culture that objectified women. He didn't like that. Not at all. But this wasn't his real job. The Casanova gig was a means to an end, and he needed to remember that. The sooner they found the saboteur, the quicker this would end.

"Casanova was a risk-taker," Quint said. "He loved intrigue and persuaded noblewomen and courtesans alike to have sex with him in dicey places. Inside a speeding carriage, or in a closet while the woman's snoring husband slept in the bed, and once, at a public execution. He was young, good-looking, well-educated and inventive and he truly enjoyed women of all shapes, sizes and ages."

"Sounds like fun to me." Troy bobbed his head.

"With the fairer sex, Casanova loved them all. No wall was too high, no gate too barbed to keep him out. When he wanted a woman, he went after her with every weapon in his arsenal and he was genuinely in love with the woman he was pursuing and his passion for her was irresistible."

"So he was a true romantic," Raoul said.

"Yes, but once a woman fell in love for him in return, he left her, just like his mother had left him. Unfortunately, Casanova didn't have the benefit of modern psychology and was doomed to repeat his unhealthy attachment patterns throughout his life." Quint paused and looked at the students.

He had them so spellbound they'd stopped taking notes and were just listening, hanging on his every word, imagining themselves as Casanova the libertine. Even the tough case, Joe, was leaning forward, ears pricked.

Lowering his voice for dramatic effect, Quint went on with the story. "There was one woman for whom he burned truly, deeply, and she drew him like a magnet."

"Who was she?" Troy asked.

"Lady Evangeline, the illegitimate daughter of Louis the fifteenth, who was also a courtesan. Lady Evangeline was the most beautiful woman at court. Every man who saw her desired her. But she was a flirtatious tease." Quint punched the PowerPoint remote control button, and the next slide featured a painting of Lady Evangeline.

"Wow, she's a hottie," said Raoul.

"Lady Evangeline led Casanova on a merry chase without ever giving in, alternately tantalizing him with seductive smiles and dismissing him with haughty snubs. She drained him of his money and power and made mincemeat of his heart. She defused him, rendered him useless, and yet he kept coming back for more. He pined for her all his life, but they never consummated their explosive affair."

"Yikes," Troy said. "I think I might have dated her."

"Sounds like someone had borderline personality disorder." Joe tossed his head back and laughed.

"That's a modern diagnosis and I prefer not to pathologize personality." Quint pressed his palms together in a single clap. "That concludes the history of Casanova. Now, we'll move on to some techniques he used to seduce his conquests. Tip number one. Appreciate her for her mind, no matter how desirable her body. She's a person foremost, not simply an object of desire."

Troy raised his hand.

"Yes?" Quint asked.

"Um, exactly how do you do that?"

"Look the woman in the eyes and listen, really listen, to what she has to say."

"Aw, man," Raoul said. "Girl talk is so boring."

"Oh, no, that's where you're wrong." Quint shook a finger at Raoul. "Listening to a woman, fulling investing in her, being honestly curious about her is the key to the kingdom, and once you know how to use active listening and reflect to her what she said, the palace is yours."

"You're going to show us how this works, right?" Troy asked.

"Yes." He nodded. "Tonight. On our gondola tour of the city."

———◦———

"LADY EVANGELINE WAS one of the most sought-after courtesans in the Venetian court," said Maggie Cantrell, the woman teaching the *Make Love like A Courtesan* course that Jorgie was enrolled in.

Maggie was as diminutive as a munchkin, pushing sixty with a strong tail wind, and she spoke in a slow, measured, deep-throated voice. "Men wrote poetry about Lady Evangeline, women wanted to be her, and children adored her. Her brains and beauty were legendary."

Maggie clicked the button to advance her PowerPoint presentation and the image of a young woman dressed in the regalia of the Venetian court in the mid-eighteenth century filled the screen. "But as you can see, she was actually not exceptional. She was, in fact, rather ordinary, but because she was so adept at the art of seduction, people saw her as a rare beauty, even though she was not."

Hmm. Jorgie leaned forward; eyes narrowed to study the on-screen image of Lady Evangeline.

"Her number one rule for bringing men to their knees was always to pay less attention to her admirer than he paid to her. For every three times he looked at her, she glanced at him once. However, if she wants the strongest seductive power over him, when their eyes did meet, she was not the first one to look away."

Jorgie jotted down this piece of advice. Interesting.

"Remember," Maggie said, "this was her advice on getting a man to fall in lust with you, not love. Love is a horse of different colored horse, and it involves far more than just sexy mind games."

"She wanted men to burn for her?" asked a woman named Callie, who was sitting next to Jorgie.

"Lady Evangeline's sexuality was her power," Maggie said. The tragedy of her life was that she would not allow herself to have the one man she truly loved."

"Who was that?" Jorgie raised her hand.

Maggie changed slides and the picture of Casanova popped up. "Giacomo Casanova. Lady Evangeline knew if she ever gave herself to fully him, she would lose the libertine forever."

"Catch-22." An older woman named Edith brushed back her long bob hairstyle from her face. "Be desired or to be loved."

"As it was," Maggie said, "Evangeline and Casanova burned for each other, but their psychology kept them apart. So if you're looking for true love, find advice from someone other than Lady Evangeline, but if you're looking to seduce, well, you can't go wrong by following her techniques."

The women in the room tittered, discussing love versus lust and how difficult it was to separate one from the other.

Jorgie listened with one ear while her mind strayed to thoughts of Quint. Would Lady Evangeline's advice work on him? Could she get him to fall in lust with her? She thought of Brian and what he'd said about her being lousy in bed and not having a romantic bone in her body.

His exact words? "You've got a calculator where your sexuality should be, Jorgie."

He'd gotten angry when she refused to buy a three-hundred-dollar French maid's costume to spice up their sex life.

Brian was right. She was not a romantic, which was why she was here. More than anything, she wanted to learn how to seduce a man with one of Lady Evangeline's come-hither looks. She wanted men to think she was beautiful, even though she wasn't.

"Don't be afraid to ignore your target," Maggie said. "Cancel a date. Stand him up. But only if you know he is already interested in you. Doing this will intrigue him further."

"What if he's the type to take 'no' for an answer?" Callie asked.

"Then breadcrumb him. We'll discuss that in a later lesson."

"Okay, what if ignoring him *does* pique his interest," Jorgie asked. "What then?"

"You'll put the poor guy into a tailspin, and he'll start wondering why you're giving him the cold shoulder him and who you're with when you're not with him."

"This sounds so manipulative." Jorgie felt uncomfortable with the idea of intentionally playing hard to get.

"All's fair in love and war," Callie said.

"Besides, you're overthinking this. We're here for a sexual fantasy. We know this is just for fun. Relax." Edith leaned over to touch Jorgie's shoulder.

Was she being overthinking this?

"Seduction," Maggie said, "is all about who has the power. Claim your power now. Chose to be in control. There is nothing wrong with that."

Several women cheered. So much for Jorgie's attack of conscience.

"Tonight, we have a flotilla of gondolas lined up to take us on an evening tour of the city and after dinner, we'll all meet outside the palace. This will be your prime opportunity to practice the skills you've learned today."

"I can't wait!" Callie wriggled.

"Dare to dress sexy," Maggie said, "show a little skin, but remember, men often feel guilty for objectifying a woman, so use good taste and common sense. Lady Evangeline had much more to give than just her body. She had a razor-sharp wit and a keen mind. She could converse on art and music and literature."

"I've got just the perfect dress for this event," Edith said. "Long-sleeved, but shows my cleavage to the max."

Maggie nodded. "For now, I want you to go back to your rooms and practice in front of a mirror sending seductive looks, and then spend some time in the museum and art gallery next to the Eros property, familiarizing yourself with the lore and allure of the eighteenth century. Class dismissed."

Heart thumping with excitement, Jorgie stood up and followed her classmates into the hallway, just as Quint's classroom let out across the corridor. Men and women converged in a cauldron of inflamed hormones. The smell of pheromones fairly wafted off the walls of the old stone building.

She spied Quint in the crowd, a head taller than most of the men.

He caught her gaze.

She held his bold stare, refusing to look away. *I'm Lady Evangeline.*

He kept ogling.

She did not blink. I won't be the first to look away.

She inhaled deeply. She could almost touch the rich air vibrating between them, the subtle scent molecules bursting—frankincense, sandalwood, sage, oak moss, nutmeg, cedarwood, black pepper. The fragrance was so thick and clear she suspected that Eros intentionally seeded the air with earthy aromas.

His gaze wavered, the smile that had started up his lips never formed. His pupils narrowed and his forehead wrinkled in a quizzical expression.

She wanted so badly to look away. Staring at him was much too intense, and she wasn't the type of person who confronted things head-on. This felt like aggression, and it made her uncomfortable. Maybe she just wasn't cut out to be a seductress.

And then Quint lowered his eyelids, and he was the first to break their gaze.

She'd won!

She barely had time to revel in the conquest when his gaze was back, looking at her with the narrowed eyes of a jungle cat.

Yipes!

This time, she would have looked away except a man even taller than Quint passed between them, breaking their eye contact. She escaped, ducking her head and slipping quickly into the ladies' room.

Blessed reprieve. This seduction business was challenging work.

She splashed her heated face with cool water and told herself to calm down. She didn't have to do this if she didn't want to. It was just a game. A bit of fun. She'd always taken sex so seriously. It was time she learned to let down her hair a little and have a blast.

Especially when she'd be having that fun time with Quint. She thought about kissing him, and her mouth went dry. Oh, how she wanted to kiss him.

Steady. Don't forget what you learned in class today. Make him want you. Act like it's no big deal.

She looked at herself in the mirror, saw her pupils dilated darkly with desire, and felt longing run through her. Tonight couldn't come fast enough.

Her heart pounded hard as she took a deep breath and stepped out of the ladies' room. She scanned the room, searching for Quint. Her eyes landed on him standing at the bar, talking to the tall man who had interrupted their eye contact earlier.

She took in every inch of Quint, admiring the way his muscles rippled in his tight shirt and how his jeans hugged his long legs, made her pulse race with desire. She could feel herself getting wet just thinking about him.

As if he sensed her staring, he turned his head and their eyes met. He flashed her a wicked grin that sent shivers down her spine.

That's when she knew she was in serious trouble.

Chapter 7

After dinner, the members of the tour group met out in front of the resort where, as promised, a flotilla of gondolas awaited them. Music poured from the outdoor speakers, "Bella Notte." People paired off two by two in the gondolas and floated away down the canals.

Jorgie had spent an hour trying on one outfit after another, struggling to find the right combination that sent the message she wanted—easy come, easy go.

She'd settled on simple tailored black slacks that fit snug and a black-and-white striped silk V-neck blouse that showed just a whisper of cleavage and black, strappy, two-inch sandals. Her jewelry was muted. Gold stud earrings and a matching gold watch. She'd bought a brighter color of lipstick than she was accustomed to wearing—Heartbreaker Red—at Avery's suggestion after she FaceTime'd her friend for advice.

Jorgie wore her hair down and ironed straight so that it swung past her shoulders. She could feel the heat of Quint's gaze on her, but she did not look over at him.

The line dwindled.

More couples paired off. She waited a full five minutes before lifting her head to meet his gaze.

The hot ardor in his eyes flattened her.

This man wanted *her*. His allure was overwhelming. She held his gaze and did not smile when he did, but lifted her chin and canted her head. She studied him with an indolent look, trying to convey that she was only mildly intrigued.

He bowed.

She nodded.

Whispered voices came from behind them, and that's when she realized his students were watching his every move. It unsettled her more than she expected.

For one thing, Jorgie had almost forgotten she was supposed to be his intentional conquest. For another thing, she'd never been one to court the spotlight.

"May I have this ride?" He extended his hand as the next gondola in line bobbed up to the loading platform.

She panicked for a second, not knowing what to do. If she refused, then she wouldn't get to ride with him. If she agreed, it would look as if Casanova's seduction techniques were working. She was supposed to be playing hard to get, but darn it, she wanted him.

Jorgie sniffed. "I wouldn't mind. Until a better opportunity comes along."

Behind them, a guy guffawed.

Quint looked a bit befuddled by her reply, but he recovered quickly. "Thank you for agreeing to accompany me."

She didn't speak, nor did she take his hand as she climbed into the boat. Instead, she held her palm out to the gondolier, who helped her inside.

Quint seated himself beside her. He smelled delicious. She darted her tongue out to lick her lips but stopped herself.

The gondolier stuck his oar in the water, and they were off, skimming gracefully across the water. The moon climbed the sky. The night breeze blew cool for midsummer, and she wished she'd worn a jacket.

Quint's knee was so close to hers. Jorgie could hardly believe she was in Venice, living her dream of a wild fling.

They glided underneath a bridge. People along the walkway overhead stared down at them. "Yo, Casanova," someone called down. "You gonna kiss her or what?"

"One of your students?" she asked.

He gave her a lopsided smile. "Sorry about that."

"You may kiss me if you wish." She leaned in closer and then paused for a moment. "For the sake of your reputation."

"That's the only reason?"
"What else would there be?"
He lowered his eyelids. "Nah."
"No?" Her stomach squeezed hard.
"I think I'll wait."
"Until when?"
"Until the time is right."

That flummoxed her. He'd looked so eager, she'd thought...

Cool it. He's not Casanova. He's just putting on a show for his students. Remember, he asked you to play the part of Lady Evangeline because you were someone he could never fall in love with.

That thought took all the wind from her sails. She turned her head, alarmed to find a salty lump in her throat.

The gondolier, a solidly built man with a broad-brimmed hat, picked up singing "Bella Notte" in a deep-throated Italian voice. Despite her best intentions to keep tight control on her emotions, Jorgie felt herself swept away by romantic Venice. She allowed the music to transport her, lost in the words and the beauty of the city.

As the gondola approached the Grand Canal, Jorgie looked to the horizon and the bright orange spots of the setting sun. The gondolier's crooning voice echoed off the canals walls, and for a moment Jorgie felt a part of something bigger than herself. She thanked the gondolier in her broken Italian and watched as the setting sun illuminated the spires of the basilicas and the timeless buildings. It was an unforgettable moment.

Quint slipped an arm around her.

Jorgie shot him a quelling glare even as her breathing sped up.

"What? Too soon?"

The line she toed was a fine one. She wanted to encourage him, but only slightly. Give him hope, but not much promise. She gave a bored sigh and looked away, much like Lady Evangeline must have done with the real Casanova beside her, but inside Jorgie's heart pounded a twitchy tempo.

The gondolier switched to "Clair de Lune" as they entered the Grand Canal thronged with gondolas. The air tasted of enchantment, impossibly sweet, and Quint's masculine scent dizzied her senses.

"This feels so magical." For a second, she forgot to be Lady Evangeline. She was all Jorgie, the girl next door, who'd spent a chunk of her girlhood fantasizing about the alluring devil-may-care man beside her. She'd imagined scenarios just like this one many times. To have him here seemed so surreal, as if she'd somehow stepped into her own daydream.

But she wasn't really here with him. Rather, she was playing a part, helping him with his class. This wasn't about a romantic evening with a man she might still had a crush on.

All the more reason to act like Lady Evangeline and keep him on his toes.

"Live the magic," Quint said.

She hadn't noticed he'd been inching his body closer, but now she saw his thigh pressed against hers and his hand had slipped from her shoulders to her waist, and that he was reaching up with his other hand to stroke her cheek before sliding it down to tilt her chin upward.

He gazed into her eyes. He was going to kiss her. She should move. Lady Evangeline would have moved.

But Jorgie was gobsmacked—by the singing gondolier, by the Grand Canal, by the full moon rising into the sky, by the dark water and the summer breeze and Quint, Quint, Quint.

Slowly, she closed her eyes, puckered her lips and waited and when his mouth touched hers, she understood the true appeal of Casanova.

He made a woman feel cherished and adored.

But was it all just an empty promise?

———◉———

QUINT'S KISS WOVE A spell over her as magical as the Venetian night—intoxicating, potent, mind-bending.

He tugged her tightly against his chest, and she did not resist. Oh, who was she kidding? She wrapped her arms around his neck and kissed him right back, as hungry as he seemed to be. Their mouths locked, oblivious to the gondolier chuckling above them.

Jorgie parted her teeth, letting him slide his tongue inside. The flavor of him, all tingling and pepperminty, filled her mouth and made her long to throw decorum to the wind and pull him down on top of her in the boat's bottom.

She'd never had such wild impulses before. What was it about him that sparked her biological bacchanal that no other man before him had ever sparked? Quint embodied the sweetest of fantasies, and she luxuriated in it, tasting it juicy as a ripe peach.

The water lapped softly against the side of the gondola like the swift swoosh of a fevered heartbeat. The ruffling breeze rippled over her bare skin, and she felt the hush of twilight settle into her soul.

She took a deep breath, smelled the Grand Canal and Quint—all fresh air and clean skin and the mossy dankness of dark water.

He kissed as the most accomplished of lovers, filled with passion and audacity and excitement. His kiss transfused those qualities into her.

He paused. His eyes gleaming with promise as he gazed into hers. He nudged her teeth apart with the tip of his tongue and lightly caressed the moistened flesh of her lower lip.

What was this magic he had about him? Not that he used his tongue in any unique way, although the tickle against the roof of her mouth set her toes curling. The pressure of his lips was firm, but not too hard, nothing earth-shattering, when you got down to it. How come it felt so exceptional?

His tongue was gentle and unhurried. Exploring, but not overstepping her boundaries the way some men did. He just teased and cajoled, tempting with a featherlight touch that intrigued. And he seemed to be truly enjoying the way she melted into him, her responsiveness fueling his own. He acted as if he could kiss her all day and never come up for air.

Heck, she ached for him to kiss her all night long!

His arms tightened around her, his chest hard against her soft breasts. Blood surged through her veins, pounded against her eardrums in the rhythm of a timeless mating ritual. Arousal was a speeding bullet shooting through her faster than anything she'd ever experienced. Instantly, she was hot and horny and hungering for him in a way she'd never hungered for another. For sure, she'd never felt this sharp, physical urgency with Brian.

Or anyone else.

She'd did not know she could feel like this. So wild and wanton and out of control. Where had it come from, this stark, primal need?

Full-throttle lust caused her to throb and ache in every molecule of her body until she was pulsing with it—her collarbone, her throat, her shins. Her skin burned, hot and jittery. Her breasts swelled heavy and sensitive against the scratchy lace of her bra, and she flushed hot all over. Not just her skin now, but she was sizzling on a cellular level—fevered, delirious, burning up with need.

He slipped a warm hand up underneath her shirt, splayed it over her belly, all the while still kissing her. Jorgie swallowed back a moan of pleasure.

You can't give in this easily. If you want to win him, then you have to make him work for it. The voice in her head dished out Lady Evangeline advice.

She leaned back, broke the kiss, and encircled his wrist with her fingers, stopping his hand from edging higher. Her mouth, wet from his kiss, cooled in the night breeze, breaking her out of the magical spell, snapping her back to reality.

"Please."

His fingers drummed lightly against her stomach, playing her like a keyboard, distracting her.

She shook her head. "Stop."

His hand stilled, but he did not move it. "You want me to stop?"

"Yes, move your hand."

"As you wish." He extracted his hand, drawing up his fingers, gliding away from her skin.

Part of her ached to invite him up to her room when they got back to the villa, but part of her knew if she gave in to him now, then she wouldn't be any different from any of the other women he'd known.

The gondolier had stopped singing, and she noticed for the first time they'd left the Grand Canal and were headed back to the villa. She heard water lapping against the boat with each stroke of the oar.

"What's going on here, Quint?"

The moonlight bathed his face in a blue-white glow. Amusement flashed in his eyes. "We're enjoying a special evening."

"Are we playing Casanova and Lady Evangelina or are you and I..."

"What?" His eyes glowed shiny in the lamplight.

"Is this thing between us pretend, or is something more going on than the alluring Venetian sunset?"

"You feel the magic too?"

Her heart thumped. Yes, yes, she did. "There's only one thing wrong with magic."

"What's that?"

"Magic isn't real."

"It's real for now."

She let out her breath, her lungs achy from holding it. "I have to know the answer. Is this about your class? About your Casanova techniques, or is this about Quint and Jorgie?"

He stared into her eyes. "It's a bit of both, I guess."

Oh, that wasn't want she wanted to hear. She wanted him to tell her it was all about her. "I'm confused."

"Casanova is part of the fantasy. So is Venice."

"That's the part that scares me. I'm a realist at heart."

"Of course, you're an accountant." His expression was both sweet and understanding.

"I don't know if I can ride on the coattails of whim and let the winds take me where they may. I don't know if I can be your conquest without my emotions getting involved."

He shrugged, and she felt it inside of her, as if she were shrugging, too. How was that possible?

"You have your whole life to be steeped in reality, Jorgie. Can't you just take this vacation as it comes? That's what Eros is all about. I thought that was why you came here."

In all honesty, she didn't really know why she was here. Mostly, it was because Avery had bought her a ticket and put her on the plane.

"I guess I'm wondering what happens when I get back home."

"You will look back on this trip with fond memories."

"That's it?"

"Why does it need to be more?" He leaned away from her. The skittish movement of a man forced to reexamine his values. "Are you looking for more?"

"I don't know."

"Do you want commitment? I thought you just got out of a relationship and wanted something different."

Jorgie sighed. "I'm not looking for happily-ever-after if that's what you're asking. I'm not even sure if I'm looking for anything at all. Still, I don't know if a romantic liaison with my older brother's best friend from high school is the right move."

He laughed and cocked an eyebrow. "Romantic liaison?"

"Okay, so I spent too much time in the eighteenth century this morning." She grinned.

He leaned in again, closing the gap he'd created, and smiled at her, his white teeth gleaming in the darkness. "It's okay, Jorgie. You don't have to do anything you don't want to do. If the fantasy isn't fun, then don't go there."

But it was fun. That was the problem. She didn't know how to have fun. She didn't know how to relax and let go. She didn't know how to be nonchalant about sex.

"Do you still want to play Lady Evangeline to my Casanova?" he asked. "Or is it too difficult to separate the game from reality?"

She bit her bottom lip. "I do want to help you with your class. I did promise and there's the free vacation…"

"I'd appreciate it, but I really I don't want you to do something you're uncertain about."

"I'm certain. Although it's all getting confused in my head. What's real? What's fantasy? What's a game? What's the truth?"

In all honesty, she wanted this. Wanted him. But she feared a broken heart. She was still raw after Brian's betrayal, even though she'd figured out she hadn't been in love with him.

That was a whole other problem.

How did you know what love was? And was romantic love anything more than just a chemical reaction? Was love itself the fantasy? One that Casanova had spent his life chasing. And how closely aligned was Quint to that famous lover?

She considered telling him she'd changed her mind, that she would love to come up to his room and spend the night having hot, sweaty sex with no consequences or repercussions or expectations. But she thought of Lady Evangeline and how the courtesan would have kept Casanova on a string by never giving in to him all the way.

The thought made her smile. How wicked it was to tease.

The gondola bumped against the landing, signaling that they'd arrived at the Eros villa. Quint got out first and then reached down a hand to help her disembark.

She took his hand because she needed his guidance, but she steeled herself against the onslaught desire.

Once she was on the cobblestone pathway beside him, she stopped and looked up at him. "Well."

"Well indeed."

The moment was awkward. She couldn't think of anything to say that would smooth it over. The evening was finished. This was goodnight. And yet, she longed to linger.

In fact, she was hoping for another kiss.

"Would you care for a nightcap in the resort's bar?" he asked.

"I don't think that would be such a—"

"Please, say yes. My students are watching and they're expecting some serious Casanova moves."

Jorgie glanced over to see a flock of young men gathered on the bridge near the entrance to the resort. They watched with knowing grins. She rolled her eyes.

"I'll owe you big time."

"All right, but only one drink and then I'm going to bed."

His grin widened. "Bed?"

"Alone," she said with added emphasis.

Chapter 8

In the darkened bar, they sat at a small bistro table in the corner. Jorgie ordered wine and Quint got a beer. Just as they were about to toast, Quint's students, Joe, Raoul and Troy strolled through the door, and grabbed a table near them, eager, he supposed, to eavesdrop on their conversation.

"Showtime." He nodded at his students.

Jorgie laughed, picking up on what he was putting down, and slanted a measured gaze at the men.

Quint scooted his chair closer to hers, his eyes sparkling with mischief as he adjust the tone of his voice loud enough for the men to overhear. "You know, Lady Evangeline, I have a confession."

Jorgie raised an eyebrow. "Oh, do tell Casanova. What could you possibly have to confess? A fine upstanding pillar of the community like yourself."

Quint sat back and clutched a hand to his heart. "I must admit, my lady, that I have been bewitched by your beauty, grace and charm. I am but a humble servant, eager to serve you any way I can."

Jorgie laughed. "That's quite a speech, Casanova. But I'm not sure I'm ready to be your mistress just yet."

The word mistress took the mood up a notch, and his body hardened. Quint leaned in again, matching his smile to Jorgie's impish grin. "Oh, my lady, you wound me! I only meant to say that I find you enchanting and that I would love to spend more time in your company."

Jorgie fluttered her lashes. "I suppose I could be persuaded to spend a bit more time with you, Casanova, but don't get any untoward ideas."

He picked up her hand and kissed her knuckles. "I would never dream of it, my lady. I grovel in your presence. I am but a humble servant, content to bask in the glow of your brilliance."

With a coy smile, Jorgie removed her hand from his. "In that case, good sir, you may accompany me to home."

His hopes leapt, even though he knew she was just playing a part and when he helped her from her chair and took her arm, he saw Raoul, Troy and Joe all three give him a thumbs up.

So far, so good. If any of them were the saboteur, he was certain they didn't suspect he was an undercover marshal.

And Jorgie had given him the perfect cover.

———— ◉ ————

AFTER HER NIGHTCAP with Quint, where Jorgie flirted and batted her eyes for the benefit of his students, who'd followed them into the bar, she allowed him to walk her to her room.

They stood in the hallway, gazing into each other's eyes. She wanted to say, ah, to heck with it and invite him inside, but she knew she couldn't. Not just for the role she was playing, but for her own emotional health.

She said goodnight, and when he leaned in for a kiss, she gathered up all the control she had in her, turned her back on him, and opened the door. She turned back to him, blocking the door with her body, and held out her hand.

"Well, goodnight."

"A handshake?" Quint chuckled.

"A handshake."

"You're killing me here, Jorgie."

"We had an agreement. One nightcap and I was going to bed alone." Then she gave him a sly smile and backed inside. Just as she shut the door, she heard a ding in the hallway as the elevator settled onto her floor.

"Hey, Casanova," she heard a young man holler. "Looks like you struck out."

She stopped the door before it closed, and cocked her head, listened to the exchange.

"I didn't strike out, fellas," Quint said as he headed down the corridor in their direction. "This is stage one in a grand seduction. It's called priming the pump. Move too fast and you'll come up dry but prime a woman right and she'll gush for you."

A snap of anger crackled through her, and she slammed the door.

Loudly.

Of all the arrogant, jerk-face things to say...

Calm down, he was only saying it for his students.

This whole role-playing thing was making her feel yanked around by her emotions. Did she want to go to bed with Quint? Did she want to learn how to have fantastic sex?

She plunked down on the bed and kicked off her shoes. She couldn't sort this out by herself. She needed someone to talk to. Mind swirling, she dug her cell phone from her purse and called Avery.

"Yo." Avery answered on the second ring. "S'up?"

"Is this a good time?"

"You mean am I having wild monkey sex with a hunky guy, then no. I can talk."

"But you said one guy had caught your eye?"

"Oh, one caught it all right," Avery said. "But he seems immune to my charms. I'm in the bungalow next to his, so I did a little striptease with the blinds open and—"

"Avery! You did not!"

"I did, but don't worry, dear Prudence, it didn't work. He saw me, I know he did, but the next day he acted like nothing had happened. Maybe he's gay."

"Or he's not the type of guy who takes advantage of horny women on vacation."

"Excuse me, but all guys are that type of guy."

"You can't paint everyone with the same brush. Some people just don't possess the same fierce sex drive you do."

"Poor them," Avery said. "So, what's going on with you? Did you have time to talk to Quint?"

"I wish you were here. I'm feeling overwhelmed." Jorgie paced the floor and unbuttoned her blouse, the cell phone cradled between her chin and her shoulder.

"Hmm, I'm sensing you took him to bed, and you turned him down."

"I had to."

"How come?"

Jorgie told her the story of Lady Evangeline and Casanova and how she was playing the part of his love interest.

"Woman, that's just whack. If you keep playing the part of this Lady Evangeline chick, you won't get any."

"I know, but I'm not sure I want to get any if it means I'll just be another notch on Quint's bedpost."

"Are you saying you want something more from him than sex?'

"No. Yes. I don't know."

"Which is it?"

"Okay, I want sex with him, but I'm afraid that if I go to bed with Quint, then I will want more, and I don't know how to stop myself from wanting more." She hung her blouse in the closet.

"So tell me what happened."

"We went on a gondola ride."

"How was that?"

"The most romantic thing I've ever done. Hands down."

"Uh-oh. That's a problem right there. Stop thinking in terms of romance. Describe it as the *hottest* thing."

"But it wasn't hot. It was romantic."

"Then stop doing romantic things."

Jorgie stepped out of her pants and hung them beside her blouse. "I'm in Venice, the most romantic city on the face of the earth. How am I supposed to do that?"

"You're working yourself up into a fuss," Avery said. "Just like you always go with guys you like."

"I don't." Jorgie unhooked her bra.

"You do, and here's the reason. You find it impossible to live in the moment. You're always thinking about the future, borrowing trouble for some time that's not even here yet. Well, what if you just found out you were going to die tomorrow? Would you sleep with Quint then?"

She didn't even have to think about it. "Absolutely."

"So there's your answer. Boink the guy until you're blue in the face."

Jorgie pulled the phone from her ear long enough to slide the bra off her shoulders and slip into her sleep shirt. "You make it sound so easy."

"That's because it is. Follow your instincts, not your brain. Your brain will trip you up every time."

"You think I should do it?"

"Do you feel safe with him?"

"No question."

"Then just go for it. Forget this Lady Evangeline nonsense. It is ancient history, and the story might not even be true. Besides, right now is all that any of us have. And even if it wasn't true, even if you had sex with Quint and despite of all your best intentions you fell in love with him and then he broke your heart, isn't it better to have loved and lost than never to have loved at all?"

————— ◉ —————

QUINT COULDN'T SLEEP.

He could still taste Jorgie on his tongue. Still smell her lovely scent in his nostrils, could still feel the effects of her in his body. The erection he'd gotten in the gondola hadn't gone away because he kept thinking about it, about her.

Restless, he left the villa and walked the cobblestones of Venice at midnight. The streets were almost empty, although there were a few couples strolling hand in hand or kissing in the moonlight. One or two drunks staggered out of bars, but mostly, he was alone with his thoughts.

And Quint didn't enjoy being alone with his thoughts.

Water lapped against the rocks. Gondolas bobbed in their moorings. He jammed his hands into his pockets; his fingers brushed against his cell phone. Jake. He could call Jake and talk about the threats made against Taylor Milton and her resorts. That ought to keep his mind off Jorgie Gerard.

"Hey, man," he said when Jake picked up the phone.

"Mason," Jake said in his clipped, all-business tone.

Anyone overhearing him would never guess that he and Quint had been friends since college, had served in the US Air Force together for four years. Jake was as reserved as Quint was open. Most people would assume they had nothing in common and on the surface, and they did not. But their shared military experience had bound them in a way nothing else could have. Their styles complemented each other. Quint was the graceful charmer, Jake, the street-savvy, tough guy.

"How are things in Lala Land?"

"Too much damned sunshine." Jake grunted. He'd been raised in Seattle and rain was as much a part of him as his taciturn nature.

"Any action on your end?"

"You talking about business or women?"

"Whatever kind of action you're getting, let's hear it."

"All quiet on the sabotage front."

"Nothing at all?"

"A chair broken in the dining hall at lunch when a hefty guy sat in it, but I think it's safe to assume it wasn't sabotage."

They'd been on this case for months now, and after the bomb that had been found in the Japanese resort, nothing else had surfaced until Taylor had received the letter.

"Did Dougal tell you about the letter Taylor Milton got?"

"He texted me a copy."

"What do you think?"

"Calm before the storm."

"That's what I was afraid of." Quint splayed a hand to the back of his neck. "Who do you think could do this?"

"My money's on a disgruntled employee, but I've been through the employee files with a fine-tooth comb and came up with nothing."

"Same here. Maybe it's the competition. Like that airline Dougal's fiancée worked for. What was it called?"

"Getaway Airlines, but Dougal put the owner, Porter Langley, through the wringer and he came up empty-handed. I hope something happens soon because I'm bored out of my skull here," Jake said.

"For real? I kind of like the quiet."

"Well, sure, you get to play Casanova. Right up your alley."

"So, how are things on the romantic front?"

"Ah," Jake said. "Sex. Your favorite topic."

"How do you have so much self-control?" Quint asked.

"Pure thoughts."

Quint laughed. "I don't believe that for a minute."

"So I take it *you're* having women trouble?"

"Not women, woman. But it's no big deal. One gondola ride and a nightcap, that's all."

Jake hooted. "She wouldn't sleep with you."

Quint felt embarrassed that he was that easy to predict.

"When was the last time *that* happened?" Jake asked.

"I don't know." He shrugged, even though Jake couldn't see him.

"Sophomore year of college. Jenny Gray. She was saving herself for marriage and she drove you crazy. You were consumed with her for months because she resisted."

"Was not."

"Dude, I was there."

"'Dude?'"

"Oh, hell. I've been in California too long and now they've got me saying it. Wish this saboteur would strike so we could catch the guy and I could get the hell out of here."

"So anyway, I need your advice. What am I supposed to do about Jorgie?"

"Stop obsessing about her."

"But how?"

"Find someone else to distract you."

"Yeah, yeah, you're right," Quint said, but he didn't want to be distracted from Jorgie but by her. All he wanted was to be with her, whether she had sex with him or not. He simply enjoyed her company.

And that scared the living daylights out of him.

Chapter 9

For seven evenings running, Jake Stewart had been treated to his own private striptease. Night after night, Avery Bodel peeled off her clothes in the bungalow's bedroom across the way. She never closed the blinds, and she always took her time.

He had to assume she knew he was watching, but during the day, when he saw her around the resort, she acted as if nothing had happened, and her mysterious little game was driving him right over the edge of reason.

Like now, for instance.

He was in the elegant dining room having breakfast with a group of camera operators, and Avery sauntered toward their table. She looked straight ahead, tray in her arms, and never turned her head in his direction, but as she passed the narrow aisle between the tables, her hip brushed lightly against his back.

Accidental? Or calculated?

Instantly, the moisture in his mouth evaporated, and his cock hardened. Someone at the table must have said something funny because everyone was laughing, but Jake hadn't heard a word. He faked a chuckle and tried to concentrate on what his colleagues were laughing about, but the only thing he was aware of was the spot on his back where her body had grazed his.

After being exposed—literally—to Avery Bodel and having the sight of her naked body burned into his retinas, he feared there was only one way to ease his burgeoning sexual appetite and get his mind back on work.

Damn his code of ethics that prevented him from mixing business and pleasure. Besides, he and Avery?

Oil versus water.

He blew out his breath and chanced a look over his shoulder to see if he could find where she'd gone. Two attractive young blondes barely over eighteen wriggled their fingers at him, then put their heads together, lowered their lashes coyly and giggled.

What the hell was going on around here?

Had someone put a Seduce Me sign on his back? Even though he didn't consider himself particularly good-looking, certainly not like his buddy Quint, and he'd had several relationships, but he'd never received this many flirtatious overtures in such a brief period. It had to be the Make Love Like A Movie Star venue. They must all be trying out the new techniques they were learning.

Each vacation tour started with the guests spending the first several days attending acting classes, touring the studios and being fitted for wardrobes. The last half of their holiday comprised starring in their own romantic movie, scripted especially for them (or they could reenacted scenes from their favorite romantic movie) to indulge their secret fantasies, but only up to a point.

The movies had to stay PG-13 rated, not crossing the lines into R or X-rated territory. However, the guests could rent cameras from the resort for their own bedroom play and in those instances, what they did behind closed doors was their business.

Most people who came on this tour were with spouses or significant others, but a few came alone looking for sexual adventures. For those guests, hired actors play the love interests. The last tour had finished up their movies yesterday and today this current group started filming. He wondered if he would be on the crew of Avery's movie or if he'd luck out and get some happily married, middle-aged couple living out their fantasies.

Jake shook his head and got up. Filming started at eight and he needed thirty minutes' prep time.

He arrived on the set along with the rest of the crew and went straight to the camera to set up the opening shot. The stagehands were already at work. Usually, the stage held a bed, but this morning, the bed had been replaced with a bathtub.

The director came onto the set, followed by his assistants, all flitting about, creating a pretty fantasy for rich people who thought nothing of plunking down cash to indulge their sexual fantasies. This glossy, insular world was a long way from the things he'd seen and done in Afghanistan. Things he'd never fully overcome.

He adjusted the camera, mentally shutting out the surrounding bustle, and wondered what it would be like to see the world as one big sexual playground, nothing but fun and games and good times.

Satisfied that he had all the settings in order, he went through the script, checking out the shots he'd need for the scene. It was pretty straightforward. They were filming the bathtub scene from *Pretty Woman* with some variations to the script that the guest had requested, including a seductive, partial striptease.

Immediately, Jake thought of the private stripteases Avery had been doing for him every night. He had to put her out of his mind. He had work to do. Both as a cameraman and as an undercover air marshal turned bodyguard for Taylor Milton's resort. From now on, he was keeping his blinds tightly closed. If Avery wanted to continue her nightly stripteases, she'd have to do it without his participation.

Then the side door opened, and Avery walked out onto the stage dressed in a bathrobe, fishnet stockings and four-inch black stilettos.

Jake's worst nightmare come true.

———————●———————

AVERY HAD REQUESTED Jake as the camera operator to film her scene. She was normally quite bold and had no trouble letting her needs be known. She was not shy or retiring, but suddenly, once she was on the stage and met Jake's eyes, her bravado evaporated.

What had she been thinking, asking for him to be the cameraman on her movie? She'd been trying for the last seven nights to drive the man crazy with sexual desire and either she wasn't doing something right or he simply was not interested in her. She should forget him. She wasn't the sort to chase after a man who didn't want her.

He wasn't involved with someone else. She'd already asked around. Maybe he was pining for an old love?

Or maybe he's just not that into you.

When she'd brushed against him in the dining room, he hadn't made a single twitch. The man had amazing self-control. She bit down on her bottom lip, just thinking about it.

"Lights! Camera! Action!"

The minute the director said those words, everyone on the sound stage sprang into motion, leaving Avery blinking into Jake's camera. She couldn't get past the fact he was there watching her, filming her. The lighting crew turned the lights on soft focus. The guy holding the boom mike positioned it over the bathtub where she would soon slide in and assume her role of Vivian, the sweet-natured hooker from *Pretty Woman*.

The tip of her nose itched, but she didn't dare scratch it.

Don't think about your nose, don't think about Jake, just enjoy this once-in-a-lifetime opportunity to be the star of your own version of this famous Cinderella story.

"Wait a minute," someone called from off the set.

"Cut." The director looked irritated. "What is it?"

The crew member went over to whisper something into the director's ear.

"Seriously?" The director shook his head.

Avery shaded her eyes against the glare of the spotlights. "Is something wrong?"

The director smiled brightly at her. "We're taking a short break."

"Is there a problem I should know about?" she asked, a knot of anxiety rising in her throat.

"Just some production difficulties. We'll be back in a minute. Tia, could you get Avery something to drink while she's waiting?"

The assistant hustled to do his bidding, while the director turned to Jake. "Stewart," he said, "I need to see you outside."

"The actor we hired for this script got a bad burrito in the cantina," said the director, Tim Granger. "We need someone to fill in for the actor."

Jake stared at the man, who kept raking his fingers through his graying goatee. "What do you mean?"

"All our actors are currently booked. We don't have time to get a temp in here. You know the script. You're good-looking enough to play the leading man, and I can get Felicity to fill in for you behind the camera."

Jake shook his head. His place was behind the camera, watching and besides, he was undercover. Being in the limelight was a stupid idea. Never mind that being that close to Avery would test every ounce of self-control he possessed.

"Not a good idea."

"Come on, dude," Tim said. "Take one for the team. You're not married, right?"

"I'm not."

"And the purple hair aside, Avery *is* gorgeous."

"Her looks aren't the issue."

"What is the issue?"

"I don't enjoy being in front of the camera."

"Get over it," Tim said. "This woman paid a lot of money to have her fantasy fulfilled and you're going to fulfill it. Get to wardrobe and makeup now."

"But..."

"Just do it."

Realizing he had little choice in the matter, Jake went into wardrobe. He couldn't decide what he was angry about, but he was. And then, as he sat in the makeup chair getting his face dusted with powder to make it less shiny under the lights, something unexpected occurred to him. He wasn't angry. He was scared.

Damn! What was he scared of?

It was a rhetorical question because he knew the answer. He feared the wild urges that hit him every time he was around Avery. He didn't like this. Not at all.

Thirty minutes later, he was backstage while the director told Avery to begin her striptease.

He could see her in profile as she eased the bathrobe off her shoulders. A wave of sensual heat shot through him, clean and deadly as a bullet. Jake sucked in a breath as his body stiffened.

Get a grip.

He tried thinking unsexy thoughts, but there was no way he could think of anything but sliding his big hands down Avery's slender body. Not when the lowering of her bathrobe kept exposing more and more skin.

"Keep it PG-13-rated." Tim Granger gave instructions to Felicity, who was manning Jake's camera to home in on Avery's legs while she dropped the towel and stepped into the warm bubble bath.

Every muscle in his body tensed as he watched her lower herself into the steamy water. She wore a tiger-print thong bikini so itty bitty it showed off the glorious body nature had given her.

All the air leaked from his lungs, and he pulled his palm down his face, searching for control. But his self-restraint had gone AWOL, leaving him aching and hungry for this woman he barely knew.

"Go." A stagehand gave him a push. "You're on."

<hr />

THE IMPACT OF JAKE'S presence on the stage sent Avery's daring spirit packing. She felt tongue-tied and owl eyed. If Jorgie were here, she'd have a good laugh.

Jake sent her a look that dizzied her head. He stared at her as if she was the only woman on earth and he was the only man and the survival of the species depended on them having sex *now*.

Avery gulped.

He came toward her, holding up the towel as she slipped out of the bathtub. She could feel the heat of his gaze burning up her skin. He wrapped the towel around her and then his arms were around her, the rolled-up sleeves of his white button-down shirt soaking up the water dripping from the ends of her hair.

His mouth closed over hers as he pulled her damp body flush against his chest. The kiss was in the script, but it felt unscripted, and he knocked the pins out from under her.

He tilted her chin with the hand that wasn't wrapped around her waist and kissed her with an open, greedy kiss so hungry it sucked all the breath from her lungs.

Avery parted her lips and his tongue slipped deeper into her mouth, running over her tongue in unabashed command. She'd thought because he liked to watch, because he hid behind a camera, that he was not a dominant, demanding guy. How wrong she'd been.

She sank against his hard body, both startled and pleased by this new revelation. His erection pushed against her belly, leaving no doubt about his interest. Luckily, his back was to the camera. He made her feel desired and wanted. It was a heady sensation.

With a soft moan, she wrapped her arms around his neck, forgetting all about the camera, the crew, the movie. Only one thing dominated her mind—*Jake, Jake, Jake.*

She pressed herself against him, trying to get closer. His mouth was still on hers, firm and inquisitive. Her sex tightened, moistening, readying for his invasion.

He splayed a palm over her rump, only the terry cloth material coming between skin-to-skin contact. Her nipples hardened in response, beading up tight, and her breath slipped from her lungs in short, escalating gasps.

Gently, he grazed her nipple, knotted stiff beneath the oversize bath towel, with the back of his hand. A sweet stinging sensation shot like a lightning bolt from her nipple to her groin, bathing her in physical awareness.

He pulled back, breaking the kiss, and peered into her eyes. An odd expression lurked in his hooded gaze—a combination of bafflement, lust, cynicism, and irritation. His breathing was as hot and fast as hers.

If the director hadn't yelled "Cut!" Avery was certain he would have kissed her again and if he hadn't, she would have kissed him.

Chapter 10

For seven days, Jorgie did her best to keep Quint at arm's length while at the same time flirting madly with him as she was supposed to do in her part as Lady Evangeline. She made sure never to be alone with him, although it wasn't easy because he seemed hell-bent on courting her.

On the day after their gondola ride, he sent her a dozen purple orchids. She had no idea how he knew her favorite color was purple or that orchids were her favorite flowers. She wanted desperately to keep them but knew that Lady Evangeline would have sent them back to Casanova with a kind note telling him she could not accept his romantic gift.

The next day, he sent her a book of erotic love poems.

She sent that back, as well, but not before she read a few of them.

The third day, he sent her a box of chocolates.

This she accepted, one because she was in truth a chocaholic and two because it's how Lady Evangeline operated. Evangeline gave in just enough to keep Casanova hooked. She heard through the grapevine that Quint crowed victoriously to his class that his techniques had battered down her defenses, but that night, at the Venetian ball, she refused to dance with him, leaving Quint looking totally befuddled.

At eight a.m. on the seventh day, both the Make Love Like Casanova and the Make Love Like a Courtesan students were scheduled to visit the island of Murano and take a private tour of a glassblowing factory. As they entered the water taxi, Jorgie held back, letting the rest of the group surge ahead and provide a protective shield between her and Quint.

She'd just sat down and looked out across the lagoon, enjoying the cool morning breeze ruffling her hair, when she felt someone sit beside her. She didn't have to look up to know it was Quint. His unique scent teased her nose.

"Hey," he said.

She glanced over at him but didn't say a word, just ducked her head, studied him through lowered lashes and tried to ignore the erratic pounding of her heart.

"You've been avoiding me." His deep voice rumbled near her ear.

"You flatter yourself that I give you that much thought," Jorgie said, trying to sound glib and carefree. Actually, she was trying to imitate Avery.

He gave her a wry, crooked smile that lit up his handsome features and splayed both palms—one on top of the other—over his heart. "You wound me."

"I seriously doubt that."

"You treat my heart so cavalierly. I do have feelings, you know, and when it comes to you, I have trouble controlling myself."

Strange emotions lumped up in her throat, knotted her chest. She stared at him, taken off guard. He sounded so sincere. She'd been infatuated with him at thirteen; she was even more attracted to him now. She'd been fighting her lust for the last seven days, but with that admission and his devastatingly adorable grin, her resolve shattered. The power of his smile set her head spinning.

Or maybe it was just the speed of the water taxi. That was it. Motion-induced dizziness. He wasn't responsible at all for the blurry, breathless sensations taking hold of her.

She leaned forward and rested her forearms on the side of the boat in an attempt to steady herself, but he followed suit, mimicking her movements, and his elbow bumped against her, firm and fundamental and so hot she felt herself melting like ice cream in the sun. It was a touch she never expected, and it sent a thrill coursing through her.

"This is fun, huh?" He grinned at her. "Being here with an old friend."

"Fun," she echoed, but the feelings churning inside her were far from fun. They were scary and exciting and nerve-racking.

"Venice is one of my most favorite places on earth," he said, his voice a low rumble in his throat.

It made her think of motorcycles and how afraid of them she was. Jorgie shifted away from his distracting elbow, sliding her arms down the smooth fiberglass of the vaporetto.

It was a beautiful day, the sky a perfect shade of baby blue, the sun bright and hot with a slight breeze to cool the air.

She felt the muscles flex in his arm as it rested on the bench. She smelled his cologne rising from him his shirt, that rich spicy scent.

She couldn't form a coherent thought when he was so close. Oh, this was bad.

"You've been here often?" she asked.

"I was stationed at Aviano Air Base when I was in the service. It's only an hour away."

"Really? I never knew you were stationed in Italy."

"For a year."

"Wow. You must have loved it here."

"I did."

They grinned at each other, and a companionable silence settled over them.

"I can't believe we're actually here," she said at last.

He chuckled, the sound sending shivers down her spine. "It's just a city like any other, Jorgie."

She turned to face him, and his eyes narrowed in amusement. "You don't believe that for a second, do you?"

He grinned, his eyes crinkling at the corners. "Okay, maybe I'm a little biased. Venice does have a certain charm but so does Murano. I came here often to visit a friend during my stent at Aviano."

"What was her name?"

"How do you know it's a her?"

"Was it?"

"Yes." His grinned widened. "Her name was Gia."

"What happened to her?"

"I honestly don't know. We weren't serious. I was just her temporary GI Joe."

"Still, it must have been romantic. Young and in love in Italy."

"Oh we weren't in love."

"No?"

"Not in the least. We were just having fun."

"But still, it's romantic."

His eyelids lowered along with his voice. "Not as romantic as being here with you."

She caught her breath, and it was only then she realized the boat had stopped moving. During their exchange, everyone else disembarked leaving them the last ones to exit.

Quint got out ahead of her and then reached down to help her out of the boat. She didn't want to take his hand, but the dock looked slippery, and she'd already seen one woman stumble. She didn't know which was the lesser of two evils—taking the risk of a fall or the risk of touching him.

Warily, she extended her palm.

His hand enveloped hers.

Their gazes met, wedded.

She shivered in response and almost yanked her hand back, but he was already pulling her up on the dock beside him.

What was going on here? Why was she letting this physical chemistry get the better of her?

"Here we are," he murmured, his voice and smile gentle as the morning breeze.

The attraction was burning too hotly, moving too fast, zooming beyond anything she could control. He was a one-man wrecking ball, crashing through all her defenses with his wickedly sexy grin.

"We're getting left behind," he said, still holding on to her hand.

She wanted to pull away but touching him felt so good. Just a minute longer, she told herself, and allowed him to lead her over the concrete walkway toward a cluster of buildings lining the main thoroughfare.

The tour guide walked ahead of the group, detailing the history of Murano. She tilted her head, trying to get her focus on what the man was saying and off the feel of Quint's calloused palm against her smooth one.

"Murano," said the guide, "is a glassmaker's paradise. The glassmaking industry was moved from Venice in 1291 because most of the structures were made of wood and glassmaking is a heat-intensive endeavor. Fearing fires could destroy the city, the town elders decided Murano was the perfect place to relocate."

They crested a small hill that descended down into the middle of town. Seagulls winged overhead, calling to each other in their squabbling voices. Vegetables, housed in wooden crates, were set up at vendors' stands overflowing with tomatoes, onions, artichokes, bell peppers and truffles. She could almost taste the tanginess of antipasto. Flowers of all colors and shapes bloomed gloriously in window boxes—jasmine, crocuses, bluebell, periwinkle and violets. The sweet, heady smell filled her nostrils as they strolled past.

But as the guide led the tour south, Quint, with his hand still wrapped around hers, steered Jorgie north.

"Where are you taking me?" she asked.

"Do you want the tourist version of glassblowing?" he asked. "Or would you like to participate?"

"What?"

"Stick with me, kid, and the world will be your oyster."

"I don't like oysters," she teased.

Truthfully, she was a bit unnerved that he was cutting her off from the herd. Not that she was afraid of him. Rather, it was her own impulses that frightened her. Alone was not a good place to be with Quint. Not when he made her feel so out-of-control.

"You'll like this," he said. "Trust me."

She glanced back over her shoulder as the other group grew smaller in the distance.

They approached a red brick building. The door stood open. The weathered sign over the door read Veneziani Glass Shop. A young man was sweeping the front stoop.

"Uberto!" Quint called.

The dark-haired young man looked up, then his face broke into a welcoming smile. "Ciao, Quint!"

They embraced, pounding each other heartily on the back. Then Uberto pulled back, peppering Quint with questions in Italian. Quint nodded and smiled.

Although she knew some rudimentary Italian, Jorgie had no idea what they were talking about, but she heard the name "Gia" mentioned and saw the young man rake a speculative glance over at Jorgie.

"Sì." Quint nodded and then motioned Jorgie over.

"Buongiomo, mancanza." Uberto waved at her and smiled.

She knew enough Italian to realize he'd wished her a good morning. Jorgie smiled back. *"Buongiomo."*

Uberto motioned them into the little shop.

Once inside, she saw a beautiful array of Murano hand-blown glass. She wanted to linger and admire the pieces with steep price tags, but Uberto motioned for them to follow him through a door at the back of the shop.

"What's going on?" she whispered to Quint.

"I've arranged private glassblowing lessons for you."

Pleased and flattered, she murmured, "That's awesome! Thank you. I'm so excited!"

The small shop opened up into a cavernous back room where the glassware was fired and formed. Two older men wearing sunglasses labored in the expansive room, handling white-hot glass with long metal tongs. The heated air carried a crisp, singed flavor that reminded her of sesame seed oil. Sweat beaded on her brow and her upper lip. She dabbed it away with the back of her hand.

"Glassblowing as an artform is over two thousand years old," Quint said. "Do you know much about it?"

"Nothing at all." She shook her head.

"It involves taking molten glass and inflating it. With help from the experts, I'll lead you through a demonstration and then you can do it."

Jorgie slapped her palm over her mouth. "Oh my, how lovely. You know how to blow glass?"

"I do. It was a side benefit of dating Gia. Uberto is her cousin."

"That's fascinating." Jorgie slanted him a sideways glance. "You're full of surprises."

"Stick with me. I've got lots of fun surprises up my sleeve." He winked.

Her heart did a little swoop and dive. How sweet of him to arrange for her to learn a new skill.

The worker in the room were fully focused on their work and offered them little more than a simple hello. Quint put a hand to Jorgie's elbow and guided her closer to the action. The heat intensified, blasting from the furnace.

"Wow," she said. "It's so hot."

"Has to be. Molten glass is viscous, allowing you to blow it, and it gradually hardens as it cools. It takes a furnace temperature of 2,400 degrees Fahrenheit to transform the raw materials into glass." He dropped his arm, and she felt the absence of his touch like a loss.

What was going on here?

Startled by her feelings, Jorgie took a lateral step away from Quint.

He didn't seem to notice and kept talking. "The glass appears white at this heat. Then the glass is left to 'fine out,' a step which allows the bubbles to rise from the mass."

"I see." But she wasn't looking at the glassblowing process as she was, rather, her gaze was fixed on him.

"And then the working temp is lowered in the furnace to around 2,000 degrees. At that stage, it will turn bright orange."

She nodded, absorbing the details. "Why are there three furnaces?"

"Good question. Glassblowing requires three furnaces at different temperatures.. The first is the crucible of molten glass. It's simply referred to as the 'furnace' and this is where it all begins."

The heat radiating from the furnace warmed her skin, even from a respectful distance away.

He motioned to a second furnace.

"This furnace called the 'glory hole', and they use it to reheat a piece that's cooled while they're working on it."

"Seriously? It's called the glory hole?" she teased and met his amused gaze.

His lips twitched. "Seriously."

"Sounds like a phrase a guy would come up with."

"You're right. It was." The smile he'd been trying to hold back, lit up his face. "Now this—" he paused and pointed out the third furnace "—is the 'annealer', and it's used to cool the glass over a period of several hours or days, depending on the size of the piece."

"Several days? Wow."

"Casanova once said that glassblowing was like making love."

"I bet." Jorgie laughed. "Casanova thought everything was like sex."

"You have mistaken idea about Casanova."

"I do? In what way?"

"He was earnestly looking for love," Quint drilled her with his gaze. "But he had an avoidant attachment due to his upbringing and never realized that the same thing he longed for was what chased him away. Once he was on the verge of finding love, he'd feel suffocated by commitment and run away."

"You paint him as a tragic figure rather than a libertine."

"Honestly, he was both. Casanova was complicated." He studied her so long that Jorgie stopped breathing. "Like most of us."

"I see."

"Casanova said that glassblowers make the best lovers."

"And why is that?" she asked, playing along, her gaze locked onto Quint's.

"Furnace number one is like good foreplay," he murmured and lowered his lashes. "Turn up the heat and melt."

Jorgie gulped. "And then?"

"It's into the glory hole."

She nudged him in the ribs with her elbow. "Pervert."

"Hey, don't blame me. I'm just paraphrasing Casanova."

"You brought it up."

He laughed and tapped the end of her nose with his index finger. "I'd forgotten how much fun you were, Jorgie Gerard."

"Okay, I'll bite. What's the last stage?"

"And then there's the afterglow of the annealer as things slowly cool down."

"So where does the blowing part come in?" She battered her lashes, noticing a bead of sweat trickling down his temple.

"How about I demonstrate?"

"Please."

He went back to the first furnace, spoke to the artisans in Italian and they moved over, making room for him to join them.

Jorgie watched as Quint got to work, donning a fireproof apron, and protective safety goggles and then picking up the tools of the trade.

His fingers were nimble on the blowpipe, and it was exciting to watch the glass inflate as he pressed his lips to the end of the tube and gently blew. His calm patience astounded her. She'd never thought of Quint as a patient person, but then again, what did she really know about the adult Quint? All she had of him were teenaged memories.

When the glass got too hot, he'd roll it against a metal table that he later told her was called a marver. When it cooled too quickly, he'd put the glass back into the glory hole for reheating. The process took some time, and she spent it utterly intrigued by the process...and by Quint.

He was creating a tiny kitten made from red glass.

"You're making a cat."

"I am."

"I love cats."

"I know."

She startled.

"Didn't you have a Siamese kitten named Mr. Buttons?"

She tilted her head, incredibly touched by both the glass kitten and his memory. "You remember Mr. Buttons?"

"I have a good memory for names." He reached for long tongs. "FYI, these are called jacks."

"Okay."

He picked up the glass kitten from the glory hole with the jacks. "And she goes into the annealer. It's such a small piece it should be ready for us to take back with us when our day on Murano is finished."

He smiled at her, so sweet and sincere, her breath hung in her lungs. At the thought of this lovely day ending, Jorgie felt wistful and wished it could last forever.

Chapter 11

U berto sauntered over and, in heavily accented in English, said, "You still have the touch, Mason. The cat is a work of art."

"Hey, all the credit goes to you, my friend." Quint shook Uberto's hand. "You taught me everything you know."

"The student becomes the master." Uberto's grin was generous.

"Not hardly." Quint rubbed the bridge of his nose with an index finger. "But thanks for stroking my ego."

"Is your lady ready for her lesson?" Uberto looked over at Jorgie.

"Oh, I'm not his lady." Jorgie took a step away from Quint.

Uberto laughed and said something to Quint in Italian that Jorgie didn't catch.

"What did he say?" she asked Quint.

"He says you can't fool him. He sees the way your eyes light up when you look at me."

Jorgie punched Quint lightly on the forearm. "He did not."

Quint threw back his head and laughed. "Can't pull one over on you, Ms. Gerard. He said *my* eyes light up whenever I look at *you*."

"Really?" Her pulse tripped over itself.

Uberto motioned them toward the first furnace.

"Come on," Quint said. "You're going to make a vase."

"Wh-what? Um... I..." Jorgie cleared her throat. Now that the time had come, she wasn't so sure about this. The furnaces were hot, and glassblowing looked tricky.

"You can't chicken out now." Quint put an encouraging hand on her shoulder. "I'm here. I've got your back."

She took a deep breath. Jorgie didn't know what unnerved her more, the idea of blowing glass or Quint.

"It'll be fun. I'll help you."

That's exactly what she was afraid of. His proximity.

"Am I backing you into a corner?" He dropped his smile. "Seriously, no pressure. If you don't want to do it, no worries. I just thought it would be fun."

"Of course, I want to do it," she said. "I do appreciate the push out of my comfort zone. Sometimes I'm a little reluctant to plunge right in."

"Do know if you change your mind, it's perfectly okay. The point is to have fun and if it stresses you out, that's no fun at all."

"Let's do this," she said, more eager now that he had given her the option to quit.

"First, we need to get you Kevlar gloves."

"But you didn't use gloves."

"You're a beginner. Trust me, you'll want them."

Uberto produced the fire retardant gloves and Jorgie slipped them on.

"Pick a cold blowpipe," Quint said and gestured toward the blowpipes arranged on a nearby metal table.

Jorgie picked up a long narrow iron tube about an inch and a half in diameter.

"Now," he said, "we go to the gathering tank."

He guided her across the room. Jorgie circled the gathering tank, feeling waves of intense, radiating heat wash over her.

"Here, let me help you." He came up behind her to show her. "Hold the rod like this."

His breath was warm against her nape as he repositioned her fingers on the cool metal rod. He wrapped his hand around her wrist and directed her forward with his leg. "Keep your knees bent."

She copied his position.

"Now, step up and set the pipe on the edge of the tank."

More heat spread over her as she followed his instructions.

"That's it. But be sure not to dip the blowpipe into the liquid glass. Just roll it over the surface until you can see the reflection of the pipe on the surface of the molten glass.

Nervously, she inched forward with a death grip on the blowpipe. Fresh sweat popped out on her forehead that has as much to do with performance anxiety as the heat. She nibbled her bottom lip, paying close attention to everything he said, and acutely aware of his chest pressing against her back.

Inside the tank, the liquid glass glowed yellow, and the heat fell over her face like a woolen blanket. She saw the pipe's reflection in the glass as Quint said she would. His hand was still on hers, helping her slowly rotate the rod.

"Two complete revolutions," he said huskily in her ear.

She rolled the pipe. She'd worked at Halloween concession stand when she was a teen and the process felt similar to turning apples in melted caramel.

"Now, carefully withdraw it," Quint murmured.

Cautiously, Jorgie removed the blowpipe from the gathering tank. The viscous glass glowed bright amber as if she'd just gathered fiery honey and it seemed to throb with the heat waves.

"I did it! I gathered molten glass!"

"Good job," he said. "But we're only getting started. Now let's move over to the marver."

From her peripheral visions, she saw the workers were watching her as she carried the blowpipe to the marver. When she reached it, Quint's arm went around Jorgie's wrist again as he helped her roll the glass into a cylinder centered on the marver.

"Okay." His voice was low, steady. "Blow into the end of the pipe and cover the hole with your thumb to trap the air inside."

Hesitantly, she put her lips to the now warm metal and blew softly, then obstructed the end with her thumb as he'd done when he made the cat. Slowly, a bubble of glass began to inflate on the other end of the rod.

"Look! Look! I did it!"

"Yes, you did." He beamed at her. "Congratulations. Step one complete. Now back to the gathering tank for more glass."

She collected more glass to add to the bubble and repeated the steps several times until Quint told her she had enough glass for the vase she was making.

"What next?" she asked, trying to remember the order he'd gone in when making the cat figurine.

"The optic mold." Quint picked up a heavy, vase-shaped cylinder and set it on the ground.

Uberto brought over a step stool and placed it next to the cylinder.

"What's this for? I didn't see you take this step," she asked.

"Beginners use a mold because it's easier," Quint said. "Experiences glassblowers use wood blocks, marvers, wet newspapers or a combination of all three to shape the form as they inflate the glass." He pointed to the two workmen who were doing just that.

"I see."

Quint helped her insert the bubble of glass she'd blown into the ribbed optic mold. "Now get up on the stool and blow an evenly spaced pattern into the glass."

Jorgie stepped up on the stool, her stomach quivering with excitement. This was so much fun! To think she'd gathered hot molten glass on a thin rod and now she was going to blow into the tube and inflate the glass into a vase. A miracle.

She put her lips to the pipe.

"Now blow. Blow, hard," Quint said.

As she blew as hard as she could, Jorgie saw the piece expanding to fit the mold. A thrill chased up her spine. Gosh, she loved this.

"Now, gently suck in to free the glass from the mold," he murmured, his hand on her shoulder. "Easy, easy."

She sucked in and the glass popped free. The glass, ribbed from the mold, glowed yellow on the end of the blowpipe.

"Let's move it over here." He guided her to two narrow metal vertical racks with a wooden bench seat in between them and helped her settle the blowpipe on it with the hot glass dangling off one rack.

The process felt so dangerous and wildly exciting.

"Crouch down on the other side of the rack and blow gently into the pipe while I help you form the glass."

She squatted and blew, moving her wrist along with the rod as Quint rolled the glass back and forth with a jack. He formed a constriction in the glass, creating a neckline for her vase.

Together, they turned the glass. She blew while he pulled and stretched with the jack. It was as if they were performing a perfect ballet, feeding off each other's energy.

"Looking good." He nodded. "Next step is to finish the shape and flatten the bottom of the vase."

"How do we do that?"

"We'll transfer the piece onto a punty for finishing."

"Punty?" She arched an eyebrow.

"It's another metal rod, but shorter than a blowpipe."

"Punty, jack, glory hole. This profession is full of sexual innuendo." She giggled.

"They don't call it the romance of Venice for nothing." Quint winked.

Umberto handed him a punty, and Quint showed Jorgie how to transfer the glass from the blowpipe. Using smaller jacks, he dropped water onto the neckline of the vase and lightly tapped the blowpipe to disconnect the glass. Then he heated the lip at the furnace and flared the opening. Jorgie watched, mesmerized.

Once he was finished, he knocked the piece off the punty and put it in the annealer for slow cooling.

"You did it," he said. "You made a vase, Jorgina Gerard."

Jorgie clapped her hands, but the sound came out muffled against the Kevlar gloves. "This is fantastic."

"I'm so proud of you." He grinned.

His kind words filled her with joy, from the bottom of her shoes to the top of her head. If she got nothing else from her Eros vacation, the trip to Murano had been worth it all.

Thrilled, she grinned and pursed her lips and leaned in close to him...

And the next thing she knew, Quint was kissing her right there in front of the glory hole.

Jorgie was taken aback for a moment, but then she melted into the kiss. His lips were soft and warm, and she felt his tongue slip past her teeth, exploring her mouth. She tasted the faint flavor of mint on his tongue, and it made her heart gallop with desire.

Without breaking the kiss, Quint took off her Kevlar gloves and ran his hands over her bare arms. His touch was electric, making her skin tingle with anticipation. Jorgie let out a soft moan as he pulled her body close to his, pressing his hard shaft against her belly.

She could feel her body soften, and she knew that she wanted him. Wrapping her arms around his neck, she deepened the kiss, letting her hands roam over his strong back and muscular arms.

QUINT BROKE THE KISS and peered down into her gorgeous face. He felt his breath leave his body and his heart contract.

Jorgie's eyes were wide, her lips wet from his mouth and her cheeks were burnished a high pink.

He didn't have to look around to know the room had emptied, because there was only silence, except for the whoosh of the furnaces and the sound of his blood pounding through his ears. Apparently, Uberto and the glassmakers had taken an early lunch to give them some privacy. He'd have to remember to thank his Italian friend for his discretion.

"Where did everyone go?" Jorgie asked.

"To lunch, I'm guessing."

"They leave the furnaces on while they're gone?"

"Yes, the furnaces must run 24/7," Quint said. "But are never left unattended. I imagine Uberto is lingering out of sight to give us some alone time while the others go to lunch."

"What do they do at night?"

"The glassblowers work in twelve-hour shifts."

"I did not know." She studied his face. "What do we do now?"

Quint smiled at her. "I've arranged for us to have a private picnic while we wait for our projects to cool."

She returned his smile, and his heart lit up as hot as the furnaces.

"Are you hungry? He inclined his head toward a wicker picnic basket sitting just inside the doorway.

"Where did that come from?" she asked, sounding delighted.

"I have my sources."

"You're trying really hard to sweep me off my feet."

"Is it working?"

"A little." She laughed.

"Come on." He held out his hand.

"Where are we going?"

"You'll see."

Just then, Umberto came back into the room, grinning like a goofball. "Buon appetite."

"Was the picnic basket your idea?" Jorgie asked him.

Umberto bowed with a flourish.

"Thank you so much."

"Enjoy." Umberto met Quint's eyes and winked.

Quint reached for Jorgie's hand, and she sank her palm against his. On the way to the exit, he picked up the picnic basket and guided her through the door into a narrow corridor and up a flight of crooked stairs.

"Where are we going?" she asked.

"To the catbird seat."

"Huh?"

"Just roll with the current, Little Bit. Do you trust me?"

"I do."

"Then come on."

At the head of the stairs was second door. Quint opened it and they stepped out onto the roof of the glass shop. The balmy breeze was a refreshing caress after the heat of the glass shop.

The roof was slightly sloped on the backside and when he spread out the blue-and-white checked cloth for them to sit on, they couldn't see or be seen from the street below. In front of them stretched the beautiful blue lagoon with water taxis gliding back and forth in the distance.

"Oh," she said. "It's beautiful up here!"

"The perfect place for a secret picnic."

"Did Gia bring you up here?" she asked.

"She did." He shot her a sheepish expression. "Is that bad?"

"No, no. It's the perfect location."

"It's so hidden by the other buildings but so open to water and sky. Romantic."

He studied her face. "It's gorgeous."

Her neck turned redder than it had when she'd been at the furnaces. "Did you and Gia make love up here?"

"We did not." He grinned at her boldness. Jorgie was loosening up. "But I like the way your mind works."

Jorgie ducked her head, reached for the basket, wishing she hadn't asked about Gia. "Whatcha got to eat?"

"I don't know. I left it up to Uberto to choose the menu. We'll find out together."

They dug through the basket like kids on a scavenger hunt, unearthing salami, a jar of olives, sun-dried tomatoes, a crusty loaf of bread and a thick chunk of cheese. They made quick work of the feast, washing it down with a bottle of red wine Uberto had tucked inside the basket, along with a corkscrew, but he had forgotten to include glasses, so they ended up passing the bottle back and forth.

"Um, are there any napkins?" she asked. "Instead of licking my fingers."

"Hmm, I wouldn't mind licking them for you." Quint wriggled his eyebrows.

She giggled, and the sound disarmed him. He wanted to pull her into his arms and kiss her breathless.

"Ah, here they are at the bottom." He handed her a napkin with a flourish. "Too bad. I was looking forward to licking your fingers."

She dabbed her fingers dry, dropped the napkin back into the basket and then she paused and slanted him a look. "The view is amazing from up here, and I just realized something."

"What's that?" he asked, her expression sending his pulse jumping.

"No one can see us up here. We're hidden behind the shop sign. That old olive tree shields us from the west, the building next door blocks us from the east. The only place where anyone could see us on this roof is from the water, and they'd have to be very close. We'd see them coming long before they saw us."

"What are you suggesting?"

"I'm thinking Casanova would take full advantage of an opportunity like this."

"Are you, now?" He slid closer to her as his hopes climbed higher. "Sexual acrobatics might be sketchy on this roof. We could slip off, fall into the water."

"That's what makes it so exciting."

"Jorgie Gerard, you little minx." Here she was issuing him a dare, a challenge, a call to adventure. Did the woman have any clue how much she stirred his blood? His body prickled with keen urgency. He'd never expected anything so audacious from sweet, innocent Jorgie. She reached for the snap on his jeans.

Spellbound, he stared, and his jaw unhinged. Adrenaline pumped through his veins as testosterone stiffed his body. Quint realized then how little he really knew about grownup Jorgie, and that sent his desire shooting even higher.

Her wicked wink sent a bolt of exquisitely excruciating lust jolting to the very center of him. He looked into her eyes, and she looked into him.

A heartbeat passed.

"I'm not wearing any underwear," she whispered.

His libido slammed into fifth gear. Then her lips, stained dark from the wine, parted and she slipped the tip of her tongue between pearly white teeth in a gesture so erotic, he almost came.

"What do you think about that?" she asked.

His gaze locked on the V between her thighs. He could not spy a panty line beneath her white shorts. Was she really going commando? Hell, did it matter? Just the suggestion lit him up, hotter than the glory hole. His mouth was dry, his stomach clenched, his brain a bundle of erotic images, all starring Jorgie.

He'd experienced no sensation like this, like her, and Quint had experienced a lot. Her fingers were still on the snap of his jeans, not undoing them, but not moving, either. His erection was granite. Who could have believed something this simple would feel so incredible? He could scarcely breathe, much less think.

Their gazes were still locked.

And Quint lost all common sense. What happened next, took his breath away.

Chapter 12

Jorgie's suddenly bold sexual confidence belied what Quint knew about her. She was sweet and a little shy. Or so he'd always thought. Then again, you had to watch out for the quiet ones. Still waters and all that. He had to admit she was a lot more complex than he knew, and he yearned to find out just more.

Hungry curiosity prodded at him. Time hung suspended. Her hand curled around his waistband, her gaze hung on his lips; the air hung rich with the heated smell of Murano, the tile roof smooth beneath his butt.

He'd started this strange dance. He was the one who'd lured her away from the group, brought her to the Veneziani Glass Shop for a very private lesson and coaxed her up on this roof for a secluded picnic.

But damn if she wasn't the one finishing it.

In the glow from the noonday sun peeping over the branches of the olive tree, he trailed his gaze from her face to her bosom, which was rising and falling rapidly as she drew in air. The red-and-white polka-dot blouse she wore molded softly to her breasts. His gaze traveled lower to her waist and beyond. The white shorts she had on snugly hugged her hips and thighs.

She undid the snap of his jeans. His erection burgeoned. She stroked him through the denim as she eased down his zipper. Quint felt his muscles contract. Then she leaned forward and nipped his chin with her teeth. Not hard, but not so soft, either.

He swallowed back a groan.

"Handling that blowpipe got me thinking."

He could smell her scent and it was driving him mad. "Yeah?"

She straddled him. His pants were unsnapped, and his zipper undone. She touched his shoulder with her palm and pushed him back against the roof. "I liked it."

"Uh-huh." He couldn't have formed a complete sentence if he wanted to. Damn, who was this woman?

She ran her tongue over her lips. "I like the feel of the pipe against my mouth. Hot and firm."

He nodded, still completely incapable of speech.

Jorgie scooted down the roof until her bottom was resting on his knees. With one hand, she pushed the hem of his shirt upward, exposing a strip of his belly to the warm sun and the cool sea breeze. It was a tantalizing combo of sensations. He loved the game she was playing. The woman was amazing.

Then she reached through the open zipper and... and... Quint's eyes rolled back in his head with sheer pleasure as she freed his erection from his pants.

"Jorgie." He panted, hardly breathing. "Jorgie."

"You may call me Lady Evangeline."

Ah, was that what she was playing at?

He grinned. Okay, fine. He reached up to touch her, to pull her head down for another kiss, but Lady Evangeline had other ideas.

She had one hand wrapped around his stiff shaft as she slowly lowered her mouth so her tongue could touch his throbbing head.

He was a goner, welded to the roof, and unable to move. He was nothing but molten glass between her nimble lips.

Around and around she swirled that wicked tongue, her instrument of pure torture. Up and down, a tantalizing, mind-blowing blend of expert maneuvers that put any courtesan to shame. What in the hell had they been teaching her in that class?

A strangled curse spill from his lips.

"That's right, Casanova, talk dirty to me."

He told her then, in very graphic terms, exactly what he wanted to do to her. He wanted to strip off her clothes, roll her over onto the roof and pour himself into the hot glory of her. He wanted to plunge and plunge and plunge until he'd fused her to him like glass to a blowpipe.

She increased the tempo of her strokes, nibbling and sucking, pulling him in and out of her succulent mouth, bringing him closer and closer to the edge of insanity. He lost all ability to think, to move from his spread-eagle position on that blue-and-white checked tablecloth on the roof of the glass shop. He felt the orgasm growing and growing and growing, hard and hot and unstoppable.

"Jorgie," he cried out. An invisible wall of water flooded over him. His body arched in an involuntary response. The sky above spun as clouds whizzed past him. It was a visual explosion of light, taste, scent, and sound.

His toes curled. His lips curled. Hell, even his hair probably curled.

A split second later, his essence spurted into the warm moistness of her welcoming mouth and his entire body went slack.

Breathlessly, Quint reached for her, intent on pulling her to his chest and telling her how much he appreciated what she'd just done for him, how he couldn't wait to do the same thing for her.

But Lady Evangeline slipped through his fingers. She got to her feet, picked up the picnic basket, and headed for the door.

"Wait, wait," he gasped, propping himself up on his elbows.

She stopped with her hand on the door, looked over her shoulder and winked at him before she disappeared down the stairs.

Holy cow, who was she becoming?

Better question, who was *he?*

———◉———

SEXUAL EMPOWERMENT quickened Jorgie's step. Wow. Just wow. She could not believe what she'd done to Quint.

She strolled down the streets of Murano, white wicker picnic basket dangling from her arm. Head held high, smiling at everyone she passed. People waved, smiled at her and called out, *"Buonpomeriggio."*

She'd never felt so strong, so alive, so in charge of her life. Taking the lead in a sexual liaison had given her unexpected self-confidence.

And even though she had the urge to check and see if Quint followed her, she never looked back. A sly courtesan would never have looked back. Lady Evangeline would never have looked back at Casanova. Looking back would make her vulnerable.

In the shop window, she saw herself. Her hair was a wild tumble about her shoulders, and she couldn't even remember when the band had broken free. A feral expression of smug satisfaction tipped up the corners of her lips stained deep pink from wine and certain illicit activities, and she found she could not stop grinning.

"You were awesome," she whispered to her reflection and fingered her bottom lip. "Nothing boring about what you just did."

Avery would be so proud of her. Jorgie had finally done something bold and daring and totally out of character. Even now, with the warm sun beating down on her and the squeak of wicker in her ears, thinking about how she'd unzipped Quint's pants and brought him to orgasm up there on the roof caused her lips to tremble and her tongue to recall the salty masculine taste of him.

Except now, it wasn't enough. She wanted more. She ached to be even bolder, even more brazen. Sexual clout, she discovered, was a very heady rush. Now she understood what Avery had been talking about all these years.

She couldn't wait to do it again.

———◦———

AFTER COLLECTING HIS scattered thoughts and stuffing his shirt back into his waistband. Quint clattered down the stairs after Jorgie, only to find Uberto and the two other glassmakers back at work.

"Did you see Jorgie come through here?"

"We saw her on the street," Uberto said. "She was smiling."

"Ciao! Thanks for letting me show her the shop and for setting up the picnic."

"Wait, don't run off so fast." Uberto went to the annealer, holding him up. He longed to race after Jorgie. "The little cat piece you made should be cool enough to take with you. The vase will take much longer to cool. I'll send it to her room at the resort with tomorrow's deliveries to Venice."

Quint shifted his weight as Uberto took the cat from the annealer and bubble wrapped it before putting the glasswork into a protective cardboard box. The entire time, he kept thinking about Jorgie.

A shudder of desire ran through him as he recalled the feel of her lips on his body. She was beyond anything he'd ever expected. She twisted him like a pretzel, working him over like an expert. He tried to tell himself he was overstating the case. That he was so impressed because it had been a while since he'd been with a woman. Especially a woman that had captivated him the way Jorgie did, but deep inside, he could not deny the truth.

Everything about her spoke to something deep within him. She struck a chord he hadn't known was there. Her sweet-yet-sexy scent, her soft voice, her ability to startle and shock him. He couldn't figure her out and he felt as if he'd been waiting his entire life to find her.

What did she think of him?

That question kept him dangling, like glass from a blowpipe—hot and ready to crack. Was he just a vacation fling for her? And if so, why did that idea bother the hell out of him? He'd never minded being anyone's vacation boy-toy before.

After a hurried goodbye, he grabbed the box from Uberto and ran from the glass shop. He couldn't wait to find Jorgie, to see her again, to figure out where this was going and what it all meant.

Quint rushed through the streets, his eyes on the lookout for a curvy brunette in a white-and-red polka-dot shirt and body-hugging white shorts with no underwear on beneath them.

At last, he spied her, standing with some of the other tourists from the Eros resort as they queued up at the vaporetto launch. She was talking to a handsome man and laughing, her face was animated.

Jealousy, sharp and quick, took a bite out of him.

He rushed up to her, even as the voice in the back of his head told him to be cool. 'There you are," he said, angling a dirty look at the guy standing too close to her.

"Hi! Have you met Ace?" She gestured toward the man. "Ace, this is Quint. Quint, Ace."

He nodded curtly. Ace stuck out his hand for a handshake, and reluctantly, Quint took it.

"Ace was telling me that Venice is sinking into the lagoon. Isn't that a travesty?"

"Tragic." He took her by the arm. "Can we talk?"

"Why, sure." Her tone was light, as if fifteen minutes ago they hadn't been up on the roof doing what they'd been doing. "What's on your mind?"

"In private." He shot a dark glance at Ace. As if that was the guy's real name.

"Okay."

His gut tightened, and he was about to direct Jorgie away from the crowd when the vaporetto docked and everyone started climbing aboard.

"Our ride is here. Looks like that private talk will have to wait." She slipped her arm from his grasp.

Quint scowled at the boat. Nothing was going as planned. He'd intended on seducing Jorgie, not the other way around. He spotted several of his students watching him. *Quick, what would Casanova do?*

"You look so beautiful." He was surprised at how heartfelt his words sounded in the languid summer air.

Her cheeks pinked, and she ducked her head. "Don't toy with me. Quint. I know I'm not a great beauty."

Maybe she wasn't a traditional beauty, but in the reflected glow of the sun off the water, Quint saw her in the same way Da Vinci must have seen Mona Lisa and been inspired to paint her. A saucy cheekiness lurked in her startling blue eyes, buried beneath the conventions of a middle-class suburban American upbringing, but it was there. She possessed a determined set to her lips that told him come what may, Jorgie was the woman you could count on.

"Oh." Her eyes widened in understanding. "You're playing Casanova for your students, aren't you? You want me to react like Lady Evangeline."

He opened his mouth, not sure of what he was going to say, when she reached out and took the box with the little glass cat nestled inside from his hands.

"For me?" She raised her voice so those around could eavesdrop. "How thoughtful." Then she leaned over and brushed her lips over his cheekbone.

That sweet kiss, that innocent kiss, that most chaste of kisses considering what she'd just done on the rooftop of the glass shop unglued him more effectively than if she'd lip-locked him in a red-hot, openmouthed kiss.

———⊙———

JORGIE WALKED DOWN the corridor toward her room at the Eros resort, the box with the little glass cat inside clutched in her hands, her mind a mad jumble.

On the vaporetto, while Quint was playing at being Casanova and she'd kissed him on the cheek, he'd had the saddest expression in his eyes. As if he were saying goodbye to an old friend he knew he'd never see again.

His melancholy expression had unsettled her. He looked as if he'd lost his best friend. Why?

He was a puzzle that was for sure.

She smiled at the memory of their rooftop rendezvous. She'd never used her sexuality to control a man before, had never understood that she could. The courtesan classes had opened her eyes to a lot of things she'd never seen before. How she'd been holding back, shutting down her natural impulses, hiding her talents.

It was long pastime she took responsibility for her sexuality, and Quint was the instrument of her rebirth. She knew she didn't have to worry about hurting him. He'd made it clear enough he wasn't a long-term relationship kind of guy. This was all about fun and learning about what she needed in bed. It was a lesson she should have learned long ago.

She'd been born cautious, but through knowing Avery, she'd learned that sometimes you had to shake things up to get noticed. That's why she was here. To get noticed and take charge of her life. To prove to Brian, and herself, that she was not boring.

Still, a part of her was scared. Afraid of getting hurt, terrified of ending up with egg on her face.

One of Avery's favorite sayings popped into her head. *You gotta break some eggs to make an omelet.* Well, if Avery knew what she'd done today, she'd have applauded.

So what next? Where did she take things from here?

Call Avery, she'll know what to do.

She dug her phone from her purse. "Guess what I did."

"No clue."

Jorgie filled Avery in about the day, from glassblowing to blowing Quint of the rooftop.

"That's wonderful!" Avery said. "Good for you."

"I never thought I'd say this but thank you for giving me the slip at the airport."

"Told you it was for your own good."

"Listen, I'm calling because I need your advice. I went out on a limb and while it was fantastic, I don't know what to do next."

"Listen," Avery said, "I'm not the best person to give love advice. Most of my relationships end after a few months."

"I'm not looking for love advice. Love is the last thing on my mind. I want to make this an epic sexual adventure."

"I'm pretty well batting zero on that score, as well." Avery paused, releasing a long exhale.

Jorgie straightened at the frustration in her friend's voice. "What's wrong?"

"Let's talk about you," Avery said.

Because she wanted to talk about what was going on between her and Quint, Jorgie let her friend off the hook. "I want to tease him. String him along. I want to make him think he has no chance of ever getting me into his bed, and then just when he's crazy with desire, I'm going to lower the boom and give him the best sex he's ever had."

"Oooh, wicked. I like it."

"So, what should my next move be?"

"Does Eros have any events planned for tomorrow night? I know our resort has evening mixers every night. Although Jake hasn't been to a single one of them."

"Who's Jake?"

"Never mind. This conversation is about you and Quint. About that mixer..."

"Um, hang on." Jorgie picked up the remote control, turned on the TV and scrolled to the resort's events screen to view the offerings. "There's a carnival mask-making competition for couples and where they compete against other teams to create the most erotic mask."

"That perfect. Not only would you be involved in a sexy craft project, but you two will work as a team in competition with others. Men love competing and doing activities together. Shared activities bond people." Avery made it sound so easy.

"Okay, I'll try it."

"Let me know how it goes."

"And you keep me posted about this Jake fellow."

"Yeah, right, that's going nowhere. Anyway, I hope you have better luck with Quint. Talk to you later." "Bye."

Jorgie switched off her phone as excitement pounded her heart. The more she thought about the erotic mask making contest, the better she liked the idea. Taking a deep breath to calm her jangled nerves, she called Quint before she lost her courage.

"'Lo." Even the way the guy picked up a call was light and breezy.

"Quint, Jorgie. I want to enter the mask-making contest tomorrow night, but I need a partner. Are you interested?"

"You and me together kicking everyone else's ass? I'm so there."

"See you in the salon at seven."

"I'll be counting the seconds," he said.

Me, too.

Chapter 13

While Jorgie was getting charged up about the mask-making competition in Los Angeles, Avery was trying to figure out why all her attempts to seduce Jake Stewart had failed.

The filming of her movie had to be cancelled when half the crew ended up suffering from food poisoning. She was left with too much time on her hands. She strolled the grounds of the resort, got a massage at the spa and talked to Jorgie, but it seemed nothing could assuage her restlessness.

When Avery got back to her room, she glanced to the open blinds of the window, and she could see straight into the window next door. Jake's blinds were open as well.

Was he there? Watching?

She squinted and thought she could see movement inside the other bungalow. Or was it just a shadow from the ruffle of curtains in the breeze?

Her breath quickened, and she felt a mesmeric force pulling her closer to the window. She was ready to take this thing to the next level. She was determined to get his attention.

"If you're over there, dude, I'm going to give you the show of your life, and even if you're not, I'm going to get an orgasm out of the deal. I've been seven months without sex and that's seven months too long."

Positioning herself in front of the window, she grabbed the hem of her cropped T-shirt and peeled it over her head. Then she shimmied from her pants, turning as she did so just in case Jake was watching. She wanted him to get a complete 360 of what he was missing.

When she'd finished, she stretched out across the foot of the bed, positioning herself so that her hair dangled over the edge, spreading out like a purple fan. She didn't care whether Jake was watching her or not. She was having a fun time all by herself. Why did she care if he hadn't responded to her nightly stripteases? There were a lot more fish in the sea.

She touched herself, trailing her fingers over her bare stomach, and thought of the way he'd smelled that day on the soundstage when he pulled her into his arms for a kiss. She could recall his clean, masculine scent. Closing her eyes, she luxuriated in the moment.

Against the backs of her eyelids, she saw Jake, the dark-eyed man she'd been unable to sway. Desire for him tugged at her. She imagined him whispering her name in his sultry, velvet-smooth voice that sent shivers down her spine.

Her heart slammed against her rib cage at the thought of Jake settling onto the soft bed beside her. Her nipples hardened and her breasts swelled. Heat pooled deep inside her.

She envisioned his hands, broad and flat, gently caressing her skin, skimming down her throat, cupping her naked breasts, moving lower, circling her navel, teasing her mercilessly.

Mewling softly, Avery used her index finger and her thumb to pinch one of her straining nipples, pantomiming what she wished Jake would do to her.

She sank her teeth into her bottom lip, eyes still closed, exploring her own body with eager fingertips. This was good. A release of sexual tension.

Her hot spine stiffened against the pillow-top mattress. Hungrily, Avery stroked the naked flesh between her thighs and all her pent-up insecurities escaped on a shattered sigh.

"Jake."

Just thinking about him and the kiss he'd given—never mind that it had been a screen kiss—made Avery feel achy and wet and hot. She traced her fingertips over tender skin, across the silky folds, skimming along the satiny moisture oozing slowly from her swollen inner core.

She pictured him with her, his caress, his hand kneading the delicate bud, dangling her on the edge of pleasure. She envisioned his mouth covering hers, his tongue nibbling, tasting, exploring. Her heart raced and her mind spun out of control.

In her fantasy, his hand dipped between her legs, caressing, rubbing her swollen sex. He drew small circles against her inner thigh with his thumb.

Her fingers moved in time with the fantasy. She was in it all the way now. No turning back. Her orgasm was so close, beckoning her onward.

Come.

Faster and faster, her fingers strummed, adding more pressure, taking her more quickly toward her goal. Release. Relief.

"Jake, Jake, Jake!" She thrashed, burning up from the inside out.

Eyes closed, she saw him looking at her with ravenous eyes, poised over her. His manhood, thick and swollen with desire, pushing against her wet flesh, sliding into her innermost cave. Dilating her, taking her, claiming her.

The orgasm ripped through her in a sudden rush. Legs stiffening, Avery arched her hips and cried out, gratification humming through her body.

She came hard, but it wasn't adequate. She wanted more. Her release, no matter how satisfying, was steeped with loneliness. The fantasy did not compare to reality. She wanted more.

She wanted *him.*

———————⊙————————

AS AVERY WRITHED IN sexual ecstasy, Jake stood in the shadows of his room, his fingernails digging into his palms. Twin impulses of aggravation and desire battled inside him. The woman was a dangerous tease. If he was a smart man, he would turn and walk right out of the room. Instead, he stayed rooted to the spot.

Clearly, he was not a smart man.

She'd gotten to him, slipped under his radar. Jake was stunned to discover how little self-control he really possessed over this woman.

It scared him.

He'd been wound tighter than wire on a spool ever since he'd kissed her on the movie set. The kiss had obviously fired her up, too.

And it took every ounce of masculine strength he possessed not to march into her bungalow, climb onto that bed with her and make love to her all night long.

Jake clenched his jaw. He couldn't, he wouldn't act on impulse. He was a controlled man, but his erection was so hard he could barely draw in air. Dammit, he wanted her.

She'd done this to him. Made him desire her in a way he'd never desired another.

He tried to think of how lust had gotten him into trouble before. But this felt like so much more than just lust. This felt *like... destiny.*

Avery turned him on and turned him inside out.

His hand strayed to the zipper of his jeans, his fingers fumbled as his breath came hard and fast. He imagined it was Avery provoking him, stroking him.

Her fantasy touch caused every nerve ending in his body to jolt with awareness as he recalled the feel of her soft lips, the sweet taste of her tongue. He visualized her long, silken curls tickling his bare skin. He saw her full, pink lips tip up in a beguiling grin.

Daydream mingled with memory as his imagination escalated the scenario playing out in his head. His shaft throbbed. His pulse raced. His brain hung on one thought and one thought only.

Avery.

Stop, stop. You've got to stop this.

But it was too late for that. His self-control was shot. He was lost. Overcome.

He stripped off his jeans and touched himself. His rhythm was frantic, desperate. He felt in equal parts embarrassment and inevitability. He had to ease the weighted need that had settled in.

Just get it over with. Quick. Empty the testosterone. Get your brain back.

He closed his eyes, took in a deep breath, and then did what he had to do to reclaim his sanity.

Avery.

A groan, half pleasure, half despair, slipped past his lips. How he wished she was the one doing this to him.

His blood pounded through his veins. There was no stopping now. What had the woman reduced him to?

And then the orgasm was upon him.

Avery.

Clenching his jaw, he shuddered as ribbons of milky heat shot up and spilled over his fist.

When it was over, he'd cleaned up, and collapsed onto the bed. In the bungalow across the way, Avery lay motionless on her bed, sated, as was he.

He could hear his own heartbeat, imagine the black, mysterious shadows of her darkened room. He inhaled it—the night—smelling thickly of his unsatisfying sexual release.

Dammit, he was here to do a job and he couldn't concentrate. He'd never been so distracted. He was supposed to be catching a saboteur; instead, fate had delivered him an unexpected complication.

Avery.

Jake draped a forearm over his eyes. He had to get his brain back. Now.

And that's when the cell phone went off that had the special ring tone he'd installed for when his boss, Dougal Lockhart, called.

Something was up.

———— ◉ ————

HAD JAKE SEEN HER? Had he watched?

Avery couldn't stand not knowing. It made irritable and antsy despite of the orgasm she'd given herself.

She thought about him in the bungalow across the way, that dark-haired, dark-eyed enigma of a man. Perspiration dewed her forehead. Her blood flowed thick with desire, and she was horny all over again.

So, had he seen her or not? Had he watched her and touched himself, as had been her intent? Or had he gone to bed, oblivious of her erotic peep show? Or... and she hated to think this... had he been shocked by her behavior and shut the blinds?

At that idea, a hot flush of humiliation burned her throat. Avery reached up to touch her lips. The kiss he'd given her on the set told her he'd been anything but disgusted, and yet she couldn't help feeling insecure. She really liked this guy. More than she'd liked anyone in a long time.

Hell, she barely knew him.

That might be true, but she couldn't help the way she felt when she was around him—alive and yet calmed, stimulated and yet soothed, energized and yet balanced. On her own, she was a spinning top. If she ever stopped, she'd fall over. Hence, she never stopped. But around Jake, she had the strongest urge to slow down and savor each second like a sinful bite of perfect chocolate cake.

So had Jake seen her and reacted, or not?

Anxiously, she swung her legs over the side of bed, pulling the sheet with her and wrapping it around her naked body. Then, holding her breath, she padded to the window and peeked across the way.

His blinds were still open.

Her heart jumped, and she moved closer, squinting in the darkness.

She spied him then, pacing the bedroom of the bungalow across the way. Buck naked, cell phone pressed to his ear.

Air leaked slowly from her lungs as she took him in. The man was beyond magnificent. The reality surpassed any fantasy she'd dreamed up about him.

His body was a work of art, no two ways about it. Had any life-form on earth had a greater impact on her? *Gorgeous* was not a good word. *Handsome* didn't begin to cover it. Even *exquisite* lacked the wonderment she felt at gazing upon this most masculine man.

Lean, but muscular. Honed and toned and tanned. Impressive pectorals, abs that put washboards to shame. A sprinkling of dark hair trailed from his upper chest down toward his abdomen. Thick, ropey veins crisscrossed his torso, a testament to a good cardiovascular system. Her fingers itched to stroke him. She wished she was closer, could see more, could trace those lines of muscles and veins, sinew and bones down, down, down to the part of him that was uniquely and utter male.

Talk about well hung! Avery licked her lips and moaned softly. Wonder what he tasted like? Earthy and rich and virile, no doubt. Salty and tangy and delicious.

She knew at once how special this moment was. The first time she saw her lover naked. She drank him in, committed every minute detail to memory.

He's not your lover.

Maybe not yet, but one way or the other, Avery was determined to make this man hers.

<hr />

"THE INCIDENT OF FOOD poisoning at the resort was not accidental," Dougal Lockhart told Jake over the phone.

"How do you know?"

Jake paced the length of the bedroom. The night air drifting in through the open window was warm against his skin. His nerves were stretched as taut as piano wire. He splayed a hand to the nape of his neck, dug his fingers into tense muscles. He was trying to listen to his boss, but his mind was on Avery.

"Taylor just got another threatening letter today," Dougal said. "I'm forwarding it to you, and he is claiming responsibility for the food poisoning."

Guilt tore at his gut. This had happened on his watch. While he'd been busy thinking about Avery and doing things he shouldn't have been doing, someone had been tampering with the resort's food supply. "You're sure it's a he?"

"No. Just using that pronoun for convenience. The culprit could easily be any gender."

"And Taylor does not know who could do this or why?" Jake asked.

"She's wealthy and powerful, and there's people who've made value judgments about what she does for a living."

"Yeah, but having an opposing opinion is one thing, taking it to this kind of extreme is another."

"I agree."

"Have we put the people closest to her under a microscope? Turned over every rock? Looked in every nook and cranny?"

"Been there," Dougal said, "repeatedly. Taylor doesn't have much family. Her husband, Daniel, who's my best friend. That's about it."

"No parents, siblings?"

"No siblings. Mother died when she was a kid. Father passed away a few years ago and left her the airline. No aunts or uncles, cousins are distant. She does have godparents."

"What about them? Could they be responsible? So often this kind of thing goes back to loved ones."

"Her godfather is General Charles Miller."

"Oh," Jake said. "Well, it's not like he'd do something like this."

"No." Dougal's sigh reverberated over the airwaves. "I'm thinking we'll never catch this saboteur."

"What do they hope to gain from this?" Jake asked. "What's their motive? Revenge for something? They're not trying to extort money from her, right? So financial gain is off the list."

"Not so far. From the gist of the threatening letters, I believe the perpetrator wants to scare her into closing down her operation. A wacko who feels sexy fantasy resorts are immoral."

"Ah, the moral crusader," Jake said.

"I know. We've looked at some people who protested her resorts when she first opened the resorts, but we came up empty-handed."

"It's frustrating."

"Yeah. Listen, just be extra vigilant. I hate to fail, and I've promised Taylor we're going to catch this guy."

"Will do. Anything going on at any of the other resorts?"

"Not so far. Looks like all the action is in L.A. Taylor is sending out a team of investigators to see if they can find out how the food got tainted, but we want to keep it on the Q.T. Don't alarm the guests."

"Gotcha."

"Remember, until proven otherwise, everyone is a suspect," Dougal reminded him.

"I always assume that." Jake's gaze drifted to the window. That meant Avery was a suspect, whether he liked it or not.

Could she be behind this? Was that why she was coming on so strong? She'd figured out who he really was, and she was toying with him?

Immediately, he dismissed that thought. He didn't know her well, but his instincts told him what you saw was what you got with Avery. From what he could tell, the woman hid nothing, but he couldn't afford to make any assumptions. Until the saboteur was located, he had to be on guard.

And then after that?

"Let me know if anything happens. If the perp hadn't taken credit for the food poisoning, we would have put it off as an accident."

"Will do."

"Good night."

"Night." Jake hit the end button and tossed his cell phone on the dresser. His gaze fell on the gauzy curtains blowing in the breeze. Tension knotted his stomach. What was Avery doing over there? Had she gone to bed? Was she still awake?

He shouldn't care. He shouldn't be thinking like this, but he couldn't seem to help himself. Like a moth to a flame, he was drawn toward the window.

Naked as the day he was born, he stepped in front of it, never expecting to find her standing at her window, staring straight at him.

Their eyes met, and their gazes locked.

His breath stilled in his lungs, and he felt an overwhelming urge to exit through the window, stalk the few short feet between them and climb into her bedroom.

Avery's sweet, perfect mouth formed a startled O.

Jake's cock hardened instantly.

Avery raised a hand, and for one stupid moment, he thought she was waving, beckoning him over. He actually stepped closer to the window.

And then she snapped closed the blinds.

Leaving Jake feeling like a fool.

Chapter 14

An array of mask-making supplies greeted Jorgie when she walked into the event room. Preformed white plaster masks had been laid out on a long folding table. There were three distinct kinds—the simple eye mask, called a *columbina;* the full-face mask, known as a *volto;* and the suggestive, long-nosed mask dubbed a *nasone* in Italian.

The art supplies lay on another table next to the one with the masks. A generous assortment of colorful feathers sprawled across one section—ostrich, peacock, turkey. There were a myriad of ribbons in every hue of the rainbow and braided trim of rich fabrics, along with Swarovski crystals, beads, buttons, and felt. The tools included scissors, X-Acto knives, primer paint, craft glue, heat guns and sandpaper.

Jorgie reached for the long proboscis of a nose mask.

"Remind you of anything?" Quint's low deep voice caused her to jump and her face to heat.

"Are you speaking as Casanova?" She battled the flush of guilty pleasure blistering her neck. Because the noses on the nasone masks looked unsettlingly like dangling male appendages. "Or Quint?"

Quint nodded at his three acolytes, who were also in the room. They'd paired up with women who were in Jorgie's courtesan classes and seemed absorbed in their own potential seductions. "Is that the mask you're going with?"

She clasped her hands behind her back. "No, of course not."

"You going with the full mask, then? Or the coquettish *columbina?*"

"Since we're a team, I thought we could choose together."

"Casanova did favor the *nasone.*"

"What a shocker, but you can stop lobbying for the *nasone.* We're not going with the penis mask."

"Jorgie! I'm shocked." An amused smile tipped his lips.

"That I know what a penis is? I thought after our time on the roof—"

"That you would say the word in public." He glanced over his shoulder at the other participants still filing into the room.

"Yeah, well, it's what everyone is thinking."

"Your boldness surprises me." He paused. "Again."

"Yeah, well, I'm learning that if you let the threat of embarrassment stop you from doing things, you'll spend your life on the sidelines. Let's go with the full-face mask." She snatched one off the table and tucked it under her arm.

"Okay." With a laugh, he followed her as she moved on over to the art supplies. Several minutes later, they found a workstation and spread out their equipment as Maggie Cantrell explained the specifics of mask-making.

"At the end of this workshop," Maggie said, "two Venetian artists who specialize in masks-making will serve as judges. The winners get use of the villa's speedboat for a private gourmet-chef prepared lunch on a nearby secluded island."

"That sounds like fun," Jorgie said. "Let's win this thing."

"You'll have an hour to complete the competition. Ready, set, start making your masks!" Maggie said.

The steps for mask-making were written on a large white board positioned at the front of the room. Plus, Maggie put on a YouTube recording featuring a Venetian mask artisan explaining the process in speaking heavily accented English.

Twenty minutes later, she and Quint were elbow-deep in hot glue and sequins and shiny glass beads. They were laughing and joking and working as a team. Amazing how much fun they were having doing something as simple as making a mask. She hadn't played like this since she was a kid.

"Does your face always light up like sunshine when you're relaxed?" he asked.

"I don't know, I don't have time to relax much."

"Your ex-boyfriend didn't do fun stuff like this with you?"

"Are you kidding? Brian was too afraid of looking ridiculous."

"You mean he would never do this?" Quint crossed eyes and stuck out his tongue.

Jorgie giggled. "Never."

"Sounds like a dullard to me."

"I was just as dull."

"Nah, you weren't dull. He inhibited you. Why were you with him?"

Jorgie paused, pondering the question.

Quint raised an index finger that had a shiny crimson button glued to it and he waggled it at her, making her giggle again. "Unless it's too painful to talk about, in which case you can tell me to mind my nosy business."

"Not much to say. He cheated on me, then blamed me for his behavior, saying I was too boring."

"What a jerk."

"The said part is, I believed what he told me."

"He was dead wrong."

"Thank you for saying so."

"I'm sorry he treated you so badly. You didn't deserve that."

"Well, he's old news. I'm here with you now."

"Yes, you are." Quint winked.

He leaned over for the hot glue gun sitting on the table beside her. His elbow brushed against her, and she knew it wasn't accidental. She gulped, suddenly filled with all kinds of feelings.

"Jorgie?"

"Yes?"

"This is me and you, right? No Casanova, no Lady Evangeline?"

He peeled the button off his index finger and for one lightning-quick second she saw heartfelt longing in his eyes, but then he glanced away.

Her heart quickened in response. "Um, could you hand me that spool of aqua ribbon?"

He passed her the ribbon.

She took it from him, pretending to concentrate intensely on the mask so she wouldn't have to deal with her complicated feelings. She dipped her head and a hank of hair fell across her face. Irritated, she pushed it behind her ears. "Dumb hair."

"What do you mean? Your hair is beautiful."

"No, it's not. It's blah brown."

"It's the color of pecan pie." He peered at her, and he was standing so close she could smell his sexy Quint scent. "I love pecan pie."

A shiver swept through her despite the warm evening.

"How about peacock feathers?" she asked, picking up one long, lovely plume. "Or should we go with ostrich? It's fuzzier, but the peacock is more dramatic." She held them up to compare.

"What are we going for here? Tactile or visual?"

"Visual is always good, but there's nothing sexier than touch." He made grabbing motions with his fingertips.

"So the ostrich?"

"Your call."

"You don't enjoy rocking the boat?" she asked.

He smiled, shrugged. "I'm easy to get along with."

"Does that make you superficial?"

One eyebrow cocked up. "You're saying I'm shallow?"

"I'm saying maybe you enjoy skimming through life on your charm and good looks."

"What's wrong with that?" he asked. "It's easier."

"You keep going whichever way the wind blows and you'll end up far from where you really want to be."

"What if I want to be where the wind blows?"

"Do you?"

He lounged against the table and studied her with heavily lidded eyes. "I don't know. Stop making me think."

"Well..." She used the heat gun to glue the ostrich feather to the mask. "What are you hanging around me for if I strain your brain?"

"You invited me to this shindig, remember?"

"That's because I thought you'd have some creative input."

He touched her hand. Their eyes met. He shook his head. "Go with the peacock feather. It's got more flash."

She put down the ostrich plume and took the peacock feather he passed her. "Thank you. That's all I really wanted."

"Just like you wanted me to kiss you at Miley Kinslow's birthday party?"

"I did not!"

Quint scooped up a handful of Swarovski crystals and canted his head, watching her glue the peacock feather to the mask with a speculative gleam in his eyes. He bounced the crystals lightly in his palm, rolled them back and forth between his long fingers. His nails were clipped short, his cuticles trimmed, and there were calluses on his fingertips. Elegant hands, but masculine, as well.

A paradox.

Here she found a complexity that belied his casual, surface demeanor. She couldn't help being mesmerized. She could almost feel his fingers on her skin. Instantly, her body grew warm and moist, and her pulse skittered.

Mischief danced in his dark eyes. "Liar. I saw you bumping the bottle with your toe trying to aim at me instead of Marty Guzman."

"You remember that?"

"I do."

"How do you remember something like that?"

"Other than you and your friend, Avery kept ogling me and giggling."

"We did not."

"You did too. Come on, admit it. You were hot for me even then." He leveled her a smug grin.

Jorgie crinkled her nose at him. "I refuse to flatter your ego."

"You had a crush on me."

"Ah, the folly of youth."

"Is that a yes? Are you admitting to a mad crush on me?"

"Are you going to help with this project or just stand there smirking?" she asked.

"The last part."

"Wrong." She pushed the scissors toward him. "Start cutting the felt."

"Slave driver."

"Slacker."

"This is fun." He beamed.

She snorted, but grinned and picked up a braided royal blue and purple ribbon. It was fun. "What do you think?"

"It matches the color of your eyes. We gotta use it."

He cut, and she glued. Fifteen minutes later, they were done. Jorgie held the mask up to her face. "How do I look?"

His eyes took on a look she couldn't describe, part awe, part desire, part amusement. "Amazing, and I should have kissed you at Miley Kinslow's birthday party, whether the bottle pointed at me or not."

That drew her up short, and she was glad she had the mask over her face to hide the blush creeping up her cheeks.

"I'm thinking I'd kiss you right now if we weren't surrounded by a roomful of mask-making folks, and Maggie Cantrell wasn't glaring at us."

"She's glaring at us?" Jorgie swung around.

"Made you look." His chuckle lit her up inside. "You are so easy. Why are you so afraid of what other people think?"

"Who says I'm afraid of that?" She sat the mask on the table and reached for elastic to make the strap for holding the mask in place.

"Come on, Jorgie, you're so busy trying to do the right thing, you don't even know *what* you want."

"Said the man who goes whichever way the wind blows."

"We're quite a pair, huh? You don't know what you want, and I don't know where I *want* to be."

His gaze homed in on her lips, then slowly eased over her chin to her throat, sliding on down to her breasts. A sweet shiver of anticipation ran through her. Instantly, her nipples hardened. Traitors.

"The judges are here." Maggie Cantrell clapped her hands to get the contestants attention. "You have a few minutes to finish up before they begin."

"You think we stand a chance at winning?" Jorgie asked, putting the finishing touches on the mask. She placed a shiny gold button to cover the base of the feathers.

He nodded. "Yeah."

"You're that confident?"

"No one has your flair with feathers, felt and glue. Look around," Quint said.

The button slipped off. "Darn it."

"Here." He leaned over her shoulder. "Let me help with that." His breath was warm on her skin. He smelled so good. Jorgie struggled to ignore the heat flaring through her.

His arms reached past her shoulders. She was trapped with him over her. He was doing this on purpose. A Casanova move. If some of his students weren't in the room watching, she might have told him to step off.

Actually, she was loving this. That was the trouble. All these fun and games had to end sometime.

He placed a huge dollop of hot glue on the mask and mashed the button into place. It held. Stupid button. "There you go."

"Everyone, bring your completed masks to the front of the room," Maggie said.

Two minutes later, with the masks arranged and the judges circling the table, Quint took Jorgie's hand in his. "Nervous?"

"Strangely enough, yes. Why would I be nervous over a silly mask contest?"

His sexy gaze raked over her. "Because you like to win."

She grinned back. "So do you."

"And because you want to spend the day with me on a deserted island."

"Cocky, Casanova."

The judges picked up the masks and inspected them closely, as if they were taking this contest way too seriously. They whispered to each other, made notes on a pad. Finally, they passed their evaluations to Maggie.

"And the winner is..."

Jorgie bit down on her bottom lip. Quint squeezed her hand.

Maggie picked up their mask. "Full-face peacock blue, created by Quint Mason and Jorgie Gerard."

"We won!" She jumped into Quint's waiting arms.

Then, in that singular moment of triumph, all the lights went off, bathing the room in total darkness.

Several people gasped simultaneously. Jorgie gave a little "Eek" of surprise. People began murmuring and bumping around.

"It's all right, everyone," Quint said, taking charge. "The generators will kick on any moment. Just stay where you are. You don't want to trip over something and hurt yourselves in the dark."

She couldn't see anything. But she could feel the hardness of Quint's honed chest beneath her fingers, and she trembled, not with fear, but with something just as elemental.

"I'm here." He tightened his strong, masculine arms around her, pulled her closer.

It was as if they were standing in the synapse of time; the world stretching out weirdly into nothingness. She could feel his steady heart thumping beneath his chest. In that instant, she felt safer than she'd ever felt in her life. Quint cupped his palm at her nape and then tilted her head upward to calm her mouth with a kiss. His lips were both hot and tender.

She couldn't help but wonder if he'd somehow arranged for the lights to be doused so that he could do this to her in the dark, in a crowded room. She could hear people shifting around them, breathing and swaying, murmuring and waiting.

Jorgie was not expecting the shocking thrill of sexual excitement that sped over her nerve endings. She felt as if everything had been switched into slow motion.

It was almost as if he could read her mind. As if their hearts were beating to the same timpani. As if his breath was hers and hers his. It was the most bizarre thing she'd ever experienced.

Something about him arrested her. Something about his calm-in-the-storm aura filled her with a keen sense of déjà vu.

She'd never felt such a compelling mental connection to any man in her life and yet it seemed so familiar, so right. Deep inside her, something monumental stirred. Something long buried. Something hoped for and dreamed of, but never acknowledged.

Soul mate.

All the caution and hesitation that had defined her life to this point vanished, and for the first time since birth, she was freed from all restrictions, all limitations. This was no mere flirtation. This was no simple tease. This was no ordinary male-female reaction.

Her skin tingled as the warmth of his breath feathered the minute hairs on her cheek. Her heart swelled. The rough material of his jacket lightly scratched her bare arm. His masculine scent soothed her.

His hard body was firm, whereas Jorgie was soft and pliable. Their mouths were frantic hunger. Her trembling increased.

"Jorgie," he murmured, breaking their kiss. "I've got you. You're all right."

His voice was thick and husky. He sounded the way red wine smelled. She thought dizzily—*cabernet, pinot noir, Syrah, merlot*. Musky and smoky, with an undercurrent of plump, tart, red sweet cherries and savory, juice-laden blackberries. A woman could get drunk on a voice like that.

On a man like this.

He held her in place, not moving, even as those around them crashed into things, cursing and complaining. She'd never thought of Quint as steady or reliable, but here he was a rock. Gibraltar. Atlas. Strong, present, unmoving. Who knew he had such depth inside him?

She heard Maggie Cantrell urging everyone to stay still and remain calm, reiterating what Quint had said earlier, promising that the backup generator would kick on momentarily. But Jorgie wanted to hear *him* speak again.

She curled her fingers around his wrist and whispered provocatively. "I'm scared."

"Nothing to be afraid of." His tone was low, measured, controlled. "You're safe with me."

His quiet, deliberate words inspired her. Where was the chatty, teasing Quint? How come he was so different in the dark?

Jorgie felt the heat of his hand at her waist, the pressure of his hip resting against her pelvis. She was disoriented, lost.

Sounds were too distant or too close, smells too sharp or too muted. The peppermint taste of him on her tongue, too sweet and too intense. The texture of his nubby jacket beneath her fingers, too authentic and yet too surreal.

She forgot about the mask-making competition and forgot they weren't alone in the room. She forgot about everything except the feel of Quint's virile arms around her and the echo of his sexy voice in her ears.

She was lost in time. Lost in the moment. Lost in the dark. The pulse at her throat kicked.

Then the lights flickered back on. The air conditioner returned to life with a stuttering hum. People applauded. And Jorgie realized something monumental. No matter how hard she tried not to, she was falling in love with Quint Mason.

Chapter 15

Quint escorted Jorgie back to her room. The place was in a hubbub over the blackout. People were wandering through the lobby talking about what they'd been doing when the lights went out. Others were at the front desk complaining. The resort manager was running around soothing ruffled feathers by offering free nightcaps to anyone inconvenienced by the loss of electricity.

He feared the power outage had been intentional, and he was eager to speak with the head of security, Frank Lavoy.

Jorgie carried the mask they'd made like a prizefighter clutching a knock-out trophy. They lingered in the doorway of her room. From the look in her eyes, he could tell she would have let him spend the night if he'd just asked, but he had work to do.

"That was some evening," she said.

"Yeah."

"Too bad it has to end." She slanted him a come-hither glance.

"On the bright side, tomorrow we've got our own private picnic."

"The bright side." She grinned.

He left her standing in the doorway, a puzzled expression on her face. No doubt she was wondering what had happened to his Casanova moves. Good. It wouldn't hurt her to wonder about him. Keep her on her toes.

A few minutes later, he found Frank in a discussion with the men from the electric company. They confirmed his fears. The fuses had been intentionally tampered with. No way could it have been accidental or caused by harsh weather.

Taylor Milton's saboteur had struck again.

Quint got little sleep. For one thing, he was up half the night—calling Dougal to tell him what had happened, dusting the electrical boxes for fingerprints, going over the details of what had happened with Frank. They'd discovered that the fingerprints on the fuse box belonged only to the maintenance staff. Either those men were involved or the person who'd tampered with the box had worn gloves.

"We've got another problem," Dougal said.

"What's up?"

"We had an incident at Jake's resort in Hollywood."

"What happened?"

Dougal told him about the food poisoning and the letter Taylor received.

"Are you saying we have two saboteurs?"

"Can't say, but one person can't be in two places at once."

"Or maybe the saboteur just contracted out his dirty work."

"Possible."

"What does your gut tell you?"

"We're being played for fools," Dougal growled.

"Yeah."

"Interview the maintenance staff. Let me know what you find."

"Will do."

Quint then spent the first part of the morning doing just that. He interviewed the staff but came across nothing suspicious. He called Dougal back to update him.

Because it was Saturday, there was no Casanova class to teach. Most of the guests had left the villa for excursions, so the lobby was empty when he finished questioning of the staff.

All except for one person.

Jorgie stood by the concierge stand, a big wicker basket draped on her arm, a wide smile on her face. She wore the sexiest pink-and-white sundress that made him think of cotton candy. He loved cotton candy.

Her shoulders were bare, save for the tiny little straps of her dress. Her glossy brown hair fell to her shoulders like a silky dark curtain. She looked gorgeous.

"Are you ready for our date?" she asked.

Date. Um, yeah. He shouldn't be going on one. Not with a saboteur on the property. But he hated to disappoint Jorgie. Dougal trusted Frank to keep an eye out. Besides, he and Jorgie would be back by mid-afternoon at the latest.

"Hang on, Jorgie. I have to make a call." He walked off to one side and phoned Frank to tell him he'd be away for a few hours and to contact Dougal directly if needed anything. He snapped his phone closed, and that's when he noticed Joe Vincent sitting at the entrance to the Internet cafe, studying him.

Joe gave him a wink and the "thumbs up" sign. Quint nodded at his student and then walked back to Jorgie.

"Ready."

The concierge gave them the keys to the speedboat moored outside the hotel and a map with detailed instructions on how to get to the island.

"You know how to drive a boat?" Jorgie asked.

He cocked her a knowing grin.

"Oh, I forgot. You're Mr. Charming. Of course you know how to drive a boat."

He got in first, took the picnic basket from her, and then reached out a hand to help her in. "And a sailboat and a race car and I can fly a plane and sky dive and mountain climb and..."

"Okay, I get it. You're worldly and accomplished. But humble? Not so much."

"I saw no reason to hide my light under a bushel, Jorgie, and neither should you." He untied the boat from the dock and then started the engine. He sat down across from her and slowly guided the craft through the narrow waterway leading to the Grand Canal. Forty minutes later, after scooting through the heavy boat traffic of Venice, they were in the lagoon heading for the small, uninhabited island.

"It says here in the guidebook that the island is haunted," Jorgie said.

"Just stuff to tease the tourists."

"I don't know. It says the island was once a penal colony."

Quint made spooky noises. "Are you afraid of ghosts?"

"No, of course not. But it sounds eerie, like Alcatraz."

"Don't worry. I'll protect you."

She snorted. "Do you think we'll have the island to ourselves?"

"Fingers crossed. Although it's probably crawling with tourists since it's Saturday."

But thankfully, he was wrong. When they reached the island, there was no one else in sight. They slide the boat onto the sandy beach and when Quint looked back, dropping anchor; he realized they could no longer see Venice.

Suddenly, the wind whipped up, dashing them with water spray. He took her arm as they passed over large, flat gray stones slippery with foam.

This time, Jorgie made spooky noises. "We're all alone on Ghost Island."

"Well, except for the ghosts."

"Look, are those the ruins of the penal colony?"

Up ahead, near a grove of cypress trees, lay a rubble of weathered gray stone. They spent the next few minutes exploring the site while Jorgie read from the guidebook.

"In the sixteenth century, the prison housed over two hundred men."

"I wonder if they were hardened criminals."

"The guidebook doesn't say."

"You hungry?" Quint asked.

"Starving."

"Let's eat."

"Where at?"

"Underneath the cypress trees?"

"Good spot."

They had to climb a small hill to reach the trees, but once they were there, they could look down on the ruins and see that on the other side lay a field of colorful wildflowers. Quint spread out the blanket they'd brought with them, and he remembered another picnic, another blanket.

"What are you smiling about?" she asked.

"I was thinking of our last outing together."

"Fun on the rooftop."

"Indeed."

"You know," she said, "I hadn't been on a picnic since I was kid, and now with you, I go on two within a week."

"Does it make you want to go on picnics with me all the time?"

"I know I'm just a summer romance for you. Don't toy with me. Don't pretend that we'll be seeing each other after this is over."

"Jorgie..." He reached out to her, not sure what he was going to say, unsure what he was feeling. He had a sudden fantasy of them. A couple. Married. Kids. The whole nine yards. Celebrating their fiftieth wedding anniversary together. It startled him, those feeling. He didn't know what it meant.

"Honestly, that's a good thing. I'm not ready for anything more than a summer fling. But you're perfect for that, Quint." She leaned over to kiss him on the cheek. "Thanks for showing me a good time."

He wanted to be closer to her. To hold her like he'd held her last night. Not to have sex—although he wanted that, hell, yeah—but to hold her in his arms and listen to the steady beating of her heart.

"Oh, look," she said, pulling food from the basket, already letting go of him, already on to the meal. "Roasted chicken and cold pasta salad."

He felt unhappy and restless, but he tried not to show it as she handed him a napkin, plastic utensils, and a paper plate. He said something he thought was funny, but he couldn't hear his own voice, his mind was humming so loudly with thoughts he'd never had before. *I want to know her better. I want to see her after this is over. I want her in my life for a long, long time.* What he said must have been funny, though, because she laughed gaily, and the sound warmed him from the inside out.

They ate, but he tasted nothing. His eyes were too full of her face. He noticed everything. The way her chin softened when she smiled. How her blue eyes shimmered like a mountain stream, how her hair ruffled lightly in the breeze. He admired the curve of her breasts underneath the crisp cotton material of her dress, and he loved the way she'd hitch up the strap on her shoulder whenever it slipped down. Her movements were so graceful, feminine, and she captivated him completely.

They sipped wine and talked for a long time. About their families, her job, his adventures. They talked about music and learned they both really liked the sound of Texas roadhouse blues—vintage Stevie Ray Vaughan, Smokin' Joe Kubek, Johnny Winter, Steve Earle and Delbert McClinton, as well as the innovative sounds of newer musical artists. The sun slipped from high in the sky, sliding down toward the western horizon. Quint was feeling content and at peace.

"This has been so nice," Jorgie said. "I really hate to leave."

"I enjoyed it, too."

"You do know how to show a girl a fun time."

"I try my best."

She smiled coyly, gathered up the remains of their picnic, and tucked it into the basket. He helped her and then folded up the blanket.

They skirted the ruins, headed toward the beach. It was a short walk and when they got there, Jorgie stopped suddenly, and he almost plowed into the back of her.

"Where's our boat?" she asked.

"It's right there..." He glanced around.

But the boat gone.

With a grunt of concern, he walked to the place where they'd beached the boat; the spot where he distinctly remembered anchoring the boat. And found a severed piece of rope with the anchor attached to it.

They weren't alone on the island. Someone had stolen their boat. But why cut the rope? Why not just pull up the anchor? He said nothing to Jorgie. He didn't want to upset her, but his mind was spinning. What if the person who'd cut the rope was still on the island with them?

———— ✦ ————

"WHAT ARE WE GOING TO do?" Jorgie bit her lip and paced back and forth in the sand.

"I'll call the resort for help." Quint pulled out his cell phone.

She scanned the lagoon, looking for signs of their errant boat, but she saw nothing except the seagulls winging their way overhead.

"I can't get a signal," he said.

"You're joking, right? Please tell me you're joking."

He shook his head. "Try your cell phone. Maybe you can better service out here."

"I left my cell phone in my tote bag. It's in the boat. We're stuck." A bubble of panic started to rise in her, but she tamped it down. She wasn't alone. Quint was here and if she had to be stranded, there was no one she'd rather be stranded with.

"It's okay," Quint soothed. "When we don't come back to the villa, they'll know something is wrong and they'll send someone after us."

"But how long is that going to take? It might be midnight before they figure out we're not there."

"It might,"

"You're saying we might have to spend the night here? On a deserted island that's haunted."

"I thought you didn't believe in ghosts."

"I don't, but it's a little easier to be brave in the daylight, when you have a boat to sail away in." Her laugh came out shaky.

"It'll be all right. We still have plenty of food. We can take shelter in the ruins. I'll start a fire. We'll make a camping trip out of it."

She smiled at him, appreciating his optimistic attitude. "You really should open a lemonade stand, the way you can deconstruct those lemons."

"Yeah, well, life's too short to dwell on the things you can't control. Come on, let's head back to the ruins."

By sundown, Quint had a fire going to provide them with light after dark. Jorgie was grateful for the warmth as well. Her thin cotton sundress did little to ward off the cool night breeze rolling in off the water.

They ate another round of roast chicken and drank the rest of the wine. After that, they sat on the blanket, their backs against the remains of the stone wall that had once formed a prison. There was no roof overhead. The fire burned just beyond their feet. They had nothing to do but wait.

"Charades? Twenty questions? Truth or dare?" Quint asked.

"Huh?" Jorgie didn't meet his eyes. She was doing everything she could to quell the urge to kiss Quint. The less she gazed into his sultry eyes, the better.

"Charades, twenty questions, or truth or dare?" he repeated, tossing a fresh log of wood on the fire. It snapped, crackled, danced higher.

"You want to play a game?"

He spread his arms wide, tilted his head up at the star-filled sky. "We're stuck here. Might as well pass the time."

"I've never been good at games."

"Well, sweetheart," he said, leveling his sexiest devil-may-care stare at her. "It's time your luck changed."

She wasn't in any condition to watch him acting out movie titles, his muscular good-looking body moving fluidly about, and the thought of truth or dare scared the pants off her. She chose the lesser of three evils. 'Twenty questions."

He sat down beside her, although a couple of feet away. "You want to go first?"

"You start. Animal, vegetable or mineral?"

"Vegetable, I guess."

"Can I put it in my mouth?"

A knowing smile tipped the corner of his lips. "Yes, you can."

"Hey, hey." She snapped her fingers. "Keep it clean."

"It is clean."

"Oh," she said, feeling equal parts disappointment and relief that his item wasn't X-rated. "But is it risqué?"

"Yes." He leveled a playful glance her way.

"Does it have anything to do with the bedroom?"

He nodded.

"Do you wear it to bed?"

"I hope so." He wriggled his eyebrows.

"Is it made of silk?"

"No."

"Cotton?"

"Nope."

"Edible underwear."

"Damn. How did you get that so fast? That was only..." He paused, counted back on his fingers. "Seven questions. You're good."

"Not really," she said. "I just understand binary search algorithms."

"Huh?"

"It's simple probability, measurable by Shannon's entropy statistics."

"Who's Shannon?"

"I'm sure you want me to skip the detailed mathematical description. Let's just say that if you know a little about statistics, you know what questions to ask. Plus, considering that the average male thinks of sex every six seconds, it wasn't too difficult to determine you were thinking about edible panties." She stroked her chin with a thumb and index finger. "I'm guessing cherry flavored edible panties."

His mouth dropped. "How the hell did you do that?"

"Please. Cherry has other connotations besides fruit flavoring."

"You're saying I'm predictable."

"Uh-huh." She nodded. "But I will admit to a secret weapon."

"Aha. I knew it. You're psychic."

"Not quite." She laughed. "My family used to play this game on long car trips."

"No fair. I've been hustled. And you said you were no good at games."

"We're all excel at something. I'm good at statistics."

"Not just good, you're a phenom. Remind me to take you to Vegas some time. We'd kick ass at twenty-one."

"That's about counting cards. Different game."

"Yeah, but they both revolve around that mathematical mumbo jumbo."

She laughed again.

"What? You think my poor mathematical skills are a laughing matter? Seriously, I wouldn't have gotten through college without Ashley Sue—" He waved. "But you don't want to hear about my old girlfriends."

"I don't," she agreed.

"How about a little truth or dare?"

"I don't know how to play."

"It's simple. If you pick truth, you have answer honestly about whatever question I ask you. If you pick dare, you have to do whatever I dare."

"I'm not sure about this."

"Oh yeah, you're Miss All That with a game you're good at, but in something 1 could best you at, you're backing off." His smile teased.

"Okay fine, truth."

"How old were you the first time you had sex?"

"Hey!" She swatted his arm. "That's personal."

"That's the point of truth or dare."

She blew out her breath. "For your information, it was my sophomore year in college. So I was nineteen."

"Late bloomer."

"Not really. I just didn't believe in sleeping with someone I didn't have feelings for."

"You're more likely to get hurt that way."

"With love, you're bound to get hurt no matter what." She shrugged. "Ever had your heart broken?"

"No."

"But I'm guessing you've broken a lot of hearts."

"I hope not." His eyes were solemn. "I've always made my intentions clear."

"You're talking the difference between the heart and the mind." She leaned forward to poke the fire with a stick, more to hide her face from him than to stir the embers.

"It's your turn," he said.

"Truth or dare?" she asked.

"Truth."

"What are you so afraid of love?"

"Who says I'm afraid?"

"You said you never gave your heart to anyone. You're almost thirty. That's just weird and come on, you make a living playing Casanova. Clearly you identify with the guy."

"You wanna know the truth?"

"Um, this is truth or dare."

He looked like he was about to confess something monumental, but then he shook his head. "I guess I'm afraid I'll mess things up."

"You probably will. You're human. We all mess up."

"Your turn again. Truth or dare?" he said.

She was tired of talking, afraid that he'd eventually hit on something she didn't want to be truthful about. Like her feelings for him.

"Dare."

"I dare you to kiss me."

The way he looked at her made every cell in her body flush hot. He rested a hand on her knee.

"Quint—"

He kissed her firmly and Jorgie took up his dare, kissing him with a fervency she hadn't known she possessed. It was raunchy, boiling, mind-bending. His arms went around her waist, and he drew her into his lap.

And the walls around her heart came tumbling down to settle among the ruins.

Chapter 16

Long days and hot nights of Casanova games and courtesan teasing heightened their hunger for each other.

Jorgie's body heated. Quint unbuttoned her sundress, just as she'd dreamed he would—one button at a time, staring into her eyes as he did it, stopping between buttons for another soul-stirring kiss.

At last, her dress was off and the cool night air, as soft as his lips, caressed her bare skin. He reached behind her and unhooked her bra. His fingers tickled.

For the first time, she saw that he was trembling, and she realized that she was, too. He dipped his head, pressed his mouth to one of her nipples, wet it with his hot tongue. She felt herself grow wetter and warmer between her legs. He played with her a moment, then went back to her lips like a honeybee at a pink peach blossom. His tongue licked hers, a fire dancing in the dark.

Joy spun her head. She pushed back the thought edging up the back of her brain that whispered she was going to regret this. That once Quint had her, that would be the end of his interest in her. But she couldn't hold out a second longer, if he walked away from this night and never spoke to her again, she would let that be okay. This savory sensation, this feeling of pure playful bliss, was worth whatever pain she might suffer later.

His kisses felt different tonight. Urgent, yet tender. Bold yet reverent.

Bumbling with urgency, she snatched at his shirt, desperate to wrestle it off him. In the end, he had to help her, shedding it over his head, tossing it alongside her bra and sundress.

She sucked in her breath at his bare, well-muscled chest. He looked powerful. Not weight-lifter bulky, but sleeker and lean. Tentatively, she skimmed her fingers over his pecs, delighting in the powerful smoothness. Had anything ever felt so good?

He kissed her again, and she trailed her arm to his back, felt the strength of his spine. His beard stubble tickled her chin. His smell, his taste, the sounds of his lips on hers, flooded Jorgie with sensation.

"Jorgie, I need you so badly."

The romance of Venice haunted her. He looked into her eyes and her heart pounded. This was it.

"I need you, too. Do you have... protection?"

"In my wallet." He stood, stripped off his pants and underwear, pausing just long enough to dig the condom from his wallet before joining her on the blanket again.

He drew her to him again. "Now, where were we?"

He rolled her over onto her back while he positioned himself over her, supporting his weight on his forearms, gazing into her eyes. The tip of his erection bounced against her belly. She laughed and the frivolous sound filled the night. His hand went to the waistband of her underwear. She raised her hips, helping him strip off her panties.

He pinned her in place and took his tongue on a trip over her body, branding her with red-hot kisses. The more she wriggled, the more he kissed and suckled, nibbled and teased.

A moan escaped her lips, and she tried to swallow it back. She was not a moaner with sex. Never had been.

"Don't hold back." His lips vibrating against her breasts. "Let it out. There's no one to hear you but me. No one to judge. Let Jorgie be Jorgie. There's no one to please but yourself Relax. Have fun. Play."

On and on, his tongue plied her with pleasure until the desire became too much for her to stand. She threaded her fingers through his hair, begged him for release, but he was relentless, bringing her just to the edge and then pulling back. She felt Uke the tide, ebbing and flowing, rising and falling.

She was helpless, frantic, floundering. He sat back. The moonlight shone on his face, bathing him in a glorious light. His erection was like a soldier, standing stiff at attention. Saluting her. Honoring her.

She parted her legs, welcoming him. "Come to me. Come to me now."

A quick rush of lavender filled her lungs when he entered her slick spot, his kisses pelting her face like hard falling rain. She squeezed her eyes closed, saw a bright burst of yellow sparkles on the back of her eyelids. Infinite motion, that's what she felt. Like the movement of air blown inside a glass, expanding, growing, flowing toward something monumental.

He was so hot inside her, molten glass. And she was the marver, cooling him down, tempering his fire. She opened her eyes and above his head; she saw a star shoot across the sky, blazing into the blue-black night.

She gripped Quint tightly with her legs.

He rocked against her, fueling the heat building, building, building inside her as she absorbed his temperature, took him in.

His body added to hers was a beautiful math, increasing friction, doubling sensation, multiplying energy.

He thrust into her, the dance they were engaged in timeless, immortal. It was sweet and wet and hot and wonderful. She reached the crest a second before he did, feeling it push her upward with excruciating delight. And then, like glass, she shattered—spinning, whirling in that split second of pure, impossible wonder.

AS QUINT AND JORGIE found paradise on a deserted island outside Venice, Avery was in Hollywood, going crazy from lack of sex. Oh, sure, she touched herself, made herself come, but that wasn't good enough. In fact, it only made her hungry for the man in the bungalow next door.

By day, the Eros film crew shot her movie with Jake as her leading man. By night, she lay in bed pining for him. Today had been excruciating. They'd filmed the love scene. It had all been covert under the covers and they'd had swimming suits on, but he'd gotten a boner and she'd been just as fired up.

It was after ten o'clock, and she was wide awake. She couldn't stop picturing his body inside hers. She threw back the covers, got dressed, slipped into her shoes. She was going over there to tell him what she wanted to do to him. She stopped in the bathroom long enough to scoop up a handful of condoms provided by the Eros resort and stuffed them into her pocket.

Her hand was on the doorknob, and she was just about to wrench it open when the doorbell rang.

Startled, she leaped back.

It rang again.

She approached the peephole. It was Jake, standing on her doorstep, looking agitated. Oh, gosh, what had she done to piss him off?

She gulped, took a deep breath, braced herself, and then opened the door.

His eyes glittered in the light from the streetlamp. He didn't say hello. He didn't ask to come in. He didn't do any of the things a civilized man would do.

Jake stepped across the threshold, took her in his arms and pulled her up tight against his chest. Avery blinked. Her blood pumped through her veins.

"Woman, do you have any idea what you've been doing to me?"

She stared into his eyes. The irises were a sharp golden brown. Tawny, like a lion. "I have?"

"Don't play coy. It's been your intention all along. Firing me up with your hot stripteases and your naughty little peepshows. I'm on to you."

"You are?" She felt breathless, dizzy. His broad, long fingers encircled both her wrists.

"You need a firm hand."

"Oh, I do, do I?"

"You know you do."

She licked her lips. It was true. She'd grown up with permissive parents. She'd been best friends with Jorgie, who always let her have her way. She tended to date playful guys who gave her anything she wanted. No one had ever really bucked Avery.

"Until now, you've been with immature guys."

Defiantly, she notched her chin upward. "How do you know that?"

"Because if you'd ever been with a responsible man, he wouldn't let you forget what a helluva woman you are. You need a challenge. You need someone who can keep up with you sexually."

Oh, my. "And I suppose you're just the man for the job?"

"I believe actions speak louder than words."

"Wha—*oh!*" Before she could react, Jake scooped her into his arms and was carrying her toward the bedroom.

It was stunningly erotic being hauled off to her bedroom. It was exactly what she'd fantasized, as if he'd read her mind, knew what was in her heart. She'd never felt like this with any man, and she'd been with more than a handful.

They weren't men. Not like this. In comparison, they were mere boys.

"Stop thinking," he said.

"What are you going to do?" she asked. "Spank me?"

"I should," he said. "For the way you've been teasing me, but I won't."

"Not even if I ask you to?"

"Not even if you begged. I don't hit women, not even in sex play."

"Aww, man."

"But I will tie you to the bedposts and lick you within an inch of your life before I take you the way you deserve to be taken."

"How's that?"

"Long, slow, hard and deep."

Her body broke out in a sweat, and she turned his head so she could crush his lips with hers. Instantly, she was slick and ready for him.

He tossed her onto the bed and bounced down beside her. His hands were all over her body, gripping and fondling with just the right amount of force. Not too gentle, not too rough. He tangled his fingers in her hair, pulled her head back for a demanding kiss. She met his demands with demands of her own, giving as good as she got.

They undressed each other, ripping and tearing, desperate to get their naked flesh pressed together.

Then he kept his promise, tying her spread-eagle to the four posts of the bed with her socks, making sure she was comfortable, that the bindings weren't too tight, before he turned his attention to teasing her mercilessly with his wicked tongue.

He kissed her many times. On the mouth, nose, cheeks and chin. He traveled lower, loving her breasts, suckling on her nipples, tantalizing her far too long before finally going down where she'd been aching for him to go.

The realization of just how much expectation she'd placed on him flooded her body with adrenaline. He drove her crazy, took her breath, stole her reason. He was so much better than she'd imagined.

An hour passed, maybe longer. She lost all track of time as he made her come again and again, licking her with his dangerous mouth. And then, when she was weak and breathless, he untied the socks and set her free. Then he kissed her, softly, tenderly, the womanly taste of her on his tongue.

"You are so beautiful, my sweet, wild thing."

That filled her with pride. He saw her for who she was, and not only did he not judge her for it, but he also appreciated her spunk and verve. She'd never known such a man.

Sheathed in a condom, he made love to her. Slow and sweet. Jake differed from other men and when she was with him, she was different.

He was changing her. Sex with him was changing her. Their games and role-playing stretched the boundaries of their identity, altering their perceptions of each other.

This man was taking her places she had never been before, carrying her into an exciting but safe harbor she'd only dreamed of A place where she felt cocooned, protected and cherished.

And she was terrified by this feeling of safety. What in the world would she do when it was gone? When he was no longer in her life?

They only had two more days together. The realization made her sad. Avery gulped. Could she be falling in love with him?

Impossible.

Unbelievable.

She barely knew him, and yet whenever he touched her or smiled at her or gave her that dark sexy look, a poignancy so sharp and sweet shot through her. Made her heart ache.

It's because he's your fantasy man. He's fulfilled your long-held secret and now you have nothing to replace it with. That's the problem. That's what's wrong.

Okay, so she wasn't in love with him. But she wanted him. Badly.

"Make love to me," she said. "I need to feel you inside me again."

"You don't have to ask twice, sweetheart." Jake reaching for another condom.

He seemed to know exactly what she needed; he'd become that attuned to her. Nothing rushed this time, nothing desperate.

His lips carried her away. His hands cherished her with caresses. Avery let herself drift, consumed by the heartfelt sadness of it all.

Nothing mattered except the moment. Not the past. Not the future. Only now.

Later, Jake shifted from long, tender thrusts to short, quicker ones.

"Yes." She squeezed her eyes tightly shut. "I like that. More. Deeper. Harder. I want you to fill me up. Please, more... give me more."

She tightened around him with each thrust and parry. Her heart pounded in her chest, in her ears, in her head, swamping her body with a heat so intense she felt as if she were literally on fire with him. For him.

He stopped moving and stared into her face. "Avery..."

"What's wrong?"

"Look at me."

She raised her lashes to peer up at him, and she could hardly catch her breath at the longing in his eyes.

With his gaze fastened on her, Jake began to move again. He filled her, wholly, completely. She had experienced nothing like the perfect union she felt with him. It wasn't his masculine power—although he certainly was strong and manly. It wasn't simply the estrogen dump from great sex. It wasn't even that they had little time left.

Rather, it was the yearning in his eyes. The solid link between them. The sensation that they were the only two people in the world.

It was all too much emotion. Too much to contemplate.

She broke the visual bond. Closing her eyes, pulling away, shutting down these feelings.

Jake thrust harder, faster. Avery mewled her pleasure. She ran her nails down his back, scratching him lightly. She wrapped her legs around his waist and clung tight. She lifted her head off the pillow and nibbled on his bottom lip.

"Almost! Don't stop!"

He pushed into her one last time, and Avery felt her sex convulse around his shaft at the same time his masculine essence shot hotly from his body and into her.

———◉———

JORGIE WOKE BEFORE dawn.

And in the muted light readying to turn purply orange she felt a sense of contentment so deep she scarcely dared breathe in fear that it would float away. She was curled into Quint, her butt tucked solidly against his pelvis, his arm thrown over her waist. The fire had burned to nothing but smoldering embers.

It was surreal, this dreamlike state, and she wondered if it all *was* a dream. The picnic. The missing boat. Their game of truth or dare that had gotten so out of hand. The unbelievably wonderful lovemaking.

It can't last. You know it can't last. He's not a forever kind of guy. You knew that when you came to this island last night. You accepted it when you got naked with him.

True enough, but that didn't stop her from wanting, wishing, hoping.

If Lady Evangeline were here, she'd tell her she'd blown it when she'd had sex with him. Keeping him on a string, teasing but never giving in, was the only way to handle a man like Quint.

But Jorgie couldn't keep doing that. For one thing, it went against her nature. For another, it wasn't fair to Quint. She couldn't change him. He was who he was, and he shouldn't be punished for it. She'd accepted her fate, now she had to live with the consequences.

It's okay, she tried to convince herself. She forced a smile, trying to make everything all right. But her heart moved leaden and sluggish against her chest.

His fingers moved, playing over her skin, making her forget everything she'd been thinking. He was awake and, from the feel, so were other parts of him.

"Mornin'." He kissed her temple. "How did you sleep?"

"Got several kinks." The cool, damp morning air demanded reverence. "And I'm sore in all the right places."

"Me, too. I haven't had a workout... a working over... like that in years."

"You saying I gave you a run for your money."

"Oh, yeah." He kissed her nape. "And then some."

"I suppose this means you aren't up to a little morning sex."

He pressed himself against her butt, his penis throbbing hard against her spine. "What do you think?"

She turned in to him. They were face-to-face, looking into each other's eyes. It felt so cozy, so intimate. She almost sighed, realizing it couldn't last.

Don't think about that, just be in the moment. She heard Avery's advice as clearly as if she'd been there saying it.

He pulled her closer, and she held on to him, so weak with lust she wasn't even worried about morning breath or how disheveled she looked. Their bodies touched from their toes to their pelvises to their foreheads. She saw the desire in his gaze, knew he was just as turned on as her.

Slowly, he stroked her, working her to a pitch as fevered and restless as the night before. He paused only to reach for a condom. When she was wet for him, he positioned himself over her and slid inside.

For a long moment, Quint didn't move. Just lay on top of her, bracing his weight on his elbows and looking into her eyes, smoothing her hair with his hands, smiling. He gazed at her as if she were the only woman in the universe.

She stared back, lost in his eyes. There was no rush like the night before. This was relaxed, playful. She could feel her own body throbbing around his hardness. She squeezed him with her inner muscles, and he let out a laugh of pure joy. It delighted her to know she'd delighted him.

Quint started moving, pumping his hips in short strokes designed to titillate. She shuddered, let out a soft moan. Pleasure gathered, closing around her like a net, pulling tight, drawing her up. The sweet pressure melted her bones, dizzied her head, took her under in a cauldron of sensation.

He nibbled her neck as he moved inside her and she writhed beneath him, pushing back against his thrusting, escalating the pleasure. She arched her hips, and he accepted her unspoken invitation, thrusting deeper, harder.

She clasped his buttocks with both her palms. "More! Faster!"

His pubic bone rubbed against her clit. Hot friction. She groaned and so did he, a guttural, masculine sound that shot her deeper into arousal.

All the while, his lips were on her face. She closed her eyes against the bliss. To feel it envelop her.

She wrapped her hands around his thick forearms roped with strong veins. Jorgie held tight to him as she fell over the precipice and into her climax.

At the same second, she felt him shudder. He buried his head against her neck, whispering, "Jorgie, Jorgie, Jorgie."

In that second she knew, no matter what happened, no matter where and how this relationship ended, she was going to love Quint Mason for the rest of her life.

Chapter 17

They dressed in awkward silence as the dawn burst wide-open. Quint didn't know what to say. Sex with Jorgie had been incredible. Unbelievable, actually, and it was nothing like anything he'd ever experienced before. The sex had been sizzling for sure, but there was more. A deeper layer. A solid familiarity. A sense of coming home after an endless journey.

Sex was different with Jorgie because she was different.

And that bothered him.

He'd told himself this was casual, that he was nothing to her but the rebound guy because that was what she needed, yet somewhere along the way he'd forgotten that and he'd allowing himself to start feeling things.

Things that could get him into a lot of trouble. Misery crawled through his body to sit heavy on his shoulders.

Every second that ticked by shortened the time they had together. Her vacation was almost over. Soon, she would fly home to Texas and he'd either be here starting a fresh Casanova class, or, if they caught the saboteur, he'd be off on a new assignment.

Once upon a time he'd viewed the Lockhart Agency as his dream job—never in one place for long, exotic cities, beautiful women, danger and intrigue. Now he was surprised to find the prospect no longer excited him. He was tired of rambling.

He'd seen the exotic cities; he'd had more than his share of adventures and he'd his fill of subterfuge and intrigue.

"Jorgie," he said, then stopped, not sure what he'd intended to say.

She turned to look at him.

The morning sun slanted across her face, casting her in a soft glow. Her hair was shiny, her eyes soft and responsive. She smiled and his heart did an odd little two-step. "It's okay. Quint, I know what you're going to say."

"You do?" How was that possible when he didn't know what he was going to say?

"We had a fun time, but that's all it was. A fun time."

"Um, right," he said, not because that was what he was feeling, but it was what she seemed to expect. "So you don't regret it?"

"Not for a second. You gave me some great vacation memories." Her smile brightened at the same time his heart sunk.

"That's good." He was lying. It did not feel the least bit good.

They stared at each other, the air practically quivering between them as they stood among the ancient ruins, and silence roared in his ears.

And all he wanted to do was kiss her again, brand her with his mouth, lick the hot pulse pounding at the hollow of her throat, but she crossed her arms over her chest and lowered her eyes.

He wanted to say something that would change everything, but suddenly he felt claustrophobic, as if the island were shrinking and the lagoon were rising and there was nowhere to run.

"Ahoy!" a man's voice called out in the distance.

It came from the beach. Simultaneous, he and Jorgie turned in that direction.

"Quint?" the man's voice echoed across the water. "Are you out there?"

Jorgie looked over at him. He saw relief in her eyes. "Sounds like we're being rescued."

"It does," he said.

"Quint! Can you hear me?" the man's voice grew louder.

Together, they ran toward to beach and found Frank Lavoy waving at them. They were saved.

Why then did Quint suddenly feel so forlorn?

------◆------

FRANK, THE HEAD OF security at Eros, told them it had taken until that morning for him to realize Quint and Jorgie were missing.

One reason for his lapse was that the boat they'd taken out ended up back at the resort, neatly tied to the dock as if they'd brought it back safe and sound. Another hiccup that got in the way was a call from Taylor Milton, announcing she was on her way back to the resort to further investigate the blackout.

Frank had called Quint's cell phone several times and had repeatedly gotten his voice mail. That's when he'd come looking. He explained all this to them as Quint and Jorgie enjoyed a breakfast of pastries and hot coffee Frank had brought with him.

One important detail stuck in Quint's head. Taylor was on her way to Venice while he'd been MIA with Jorgie. She was scheduled to arrive soon.

Guilt bit into him. He'd fallen down on the job. He knew he shouldn't have gone on the picnic with Jorgie, but he'd been unable to help himself. She'd bewitched him, this sweet girl-next-door with a deliciously wicked side. And he was going to have to pay the price, but, man, what a glorious way to fall.

He'd make it up to Taylor any way he could.

They reached the resort forty minutes after Frank rescued them. He had Jorgie's tote bag, that he'd found in the boat, with him and he gave it to her. She went through it. Everything was there—her ID, cell phone, money, and credit cards. Nothing had been taken.

Jorgie thanked Frank for rescuing them, and then she mumbled something about a shower and took off inside the resort.

Quint wanted to go with her, but Frank clamped a hand on his shoulder. Once Jorgie was out of earshot, he said, "Damn, I'm glad you're okay. What happened out there?"

Quickly, Quint told him what had transpired on the island the previous day, including that the anchor rope had been cut. "The culprit could have just pulled up the anchor. Cutting the rope tells me that whoever they were was sending a message.

"I agree," Frank said. "Someone wanted you to know they'd intentionally stranded you to keep you out of the way."

"Looks like it. Did anything happen last night while we were gone?"

Frank shook his head. "Not that I'm aware of."

Quint stroked his jaw with his thumb and forefinger. "This smells fishy. How are things this morning?"

"Other than me realizing you'd going missing and Taylor on the way? Quiet. It is Sunday. Most people are sleeping in or attending the festival at the Piazza San Marco."

"I've got a bad feeling about this whole thing. I think maybe there's more trouble in the offing."

"Me, too. I called in everyone on their day off. We're loaded for bear."

"That's good. When's Taylor scheduled to arrive?"

Frank consulted his watch. "Within the next hour."

"With your entire staff on board that gives us just enough time to do a sweep of the place."

"What exactly are we looking for?" Frank asked.

Quint met his gaze. "All signs of trouble."

Frank snorted. "That narrows it down."

"Yeah, I get it's a monumental task, so let's get to it."

———— ◉ ————

JORGIE ENTERED THE lobby just as her cell phone rang. She was tempted to let it go to voice mail and call Avery back later, but she wanted to tell her friend what had happened on the island and get her advice on how to handle her strung out feelings.

She plunked down on a plush sofa in the lobby and opened her phone. The battery was low. Just twenty percent power left. She needed to get it on a charger.

"What time is it in L. A?" she asked.

"I'm nine hours behind you," Avery said.

"So it's around midnight where you are. What's up?"

"You will not believe this."

She could hear something different in her friend's voice. Something reverential, sacred. "What's happened?"

"Are you sitting down?"

Jorgie plopped down into a lobby chair. "Yes."

"I'm in love," Avery squeaked.

That was the last thing on earth Jorgie ever expected her friend to say. "What?"

"Oh, Jorgie, I never knew I could feel this way. It's wonderful, breathtaking. I feel like a new person. I feel like the world is wide open with possibilities. I feel..." Avery paused, inhaled audibly. "I feel so damn much I can't express it all."

Jorgie bit down on her bottom lip to keep it from trembling. She knew how that felt, too. Except her joy was colored with darkness because she was uncertain about the future. "What's his name?"

"It's Jake, and he's magnificent." Then Avery was off, chatting about the hunky Eros cameraman who'd captured her heart.

Jorgie just listened, offering no advice.

"So how are things with you and Quint?" Avery asked when she finally took a breath..

"He's fine," Jorgie said, no longer to talk about Quint. Not in the face of Avery's over-the-top joy.

"Did you guys ever hook up?"

"We did."

"How do you feel?"

A mass of emotions tangled up in Jorgie like short-circuiting wires. She didn't think she could talk about it without crying. "Look, Av, can I call you back?"

"Sure, sure, but make it later. Much later. I'm going back to bed and snuggling up next to Jake."

"That's wonderful. Enjoy yourself."

"I will! He's a top-notch cuddler."

"Goodnight." Jorgie ended the call. She stuffed her phone back into her tote, grabbed her key card from the side pocket of the bag, and headed for her room. She couldn't wait to get into the shower, where she could have a good, long, hot, wet sob fest.

Jorgie was so caught up in her mental turmoil of her future—or lack thereof—with Quint that she paid little attention to her surroundings. She had just unlocked the door open, and her head was down.

She didn't see danger lurking.

One minute she was on her feet thinking about Quint and her life and the fork in the road she was facing...

Then *boom!*

She was lying on the cool marble tile watching someone dressed all in black and wearing a black ski mask step over her body and sprint out the door. It took a second or two for her mind to register what had just happened.

Someone had been in her room, and they'd just plowed into her as they made their escape, knocking her to the ground.

She lay there on the floor, head throbbing, fear pressing down hard on her lungs, squeezing out the delayed sound of the scream she hadn't even known she'd screamed.

———————◉———————

JORGIE!

Quint was headed for the elevators when he heard the scream that curdled his blood echo throughout the open atrium, and he knew instantly it was Jorgie.

Get to her now!

Instinct and training had him rushing for the hallway just as a figure dressed all in black barreled past him and ran through the lobby. He wished he had his duty weapon. He'd left it behind when he'd gone on the picnic with Jorgie. Another dumb move in an extensive line of dumb moves.

Several of the guests gasped as the person in black spun through the crowd lined up at the registration desk.

For a split second, he was hung on the horns of indecision. Should he go after the suspicious-looking character in black or make sure Jorgie was okay?

"Stop!" Quint yelled.

To his surprise, the figure in black halted, but only for a fleeting moment. Then they turned and fled through the side door, knocking over an elderly woman.

Quint's instincts urged him to give chase. But the thought of Jorgie lying hurt, or bleeding obscured everything else. He'd never been in a position like this. Having to choose duty over a loved one.

Loved one.

The words etched into his brain.

It was no contest.

Eschewing the elevator for the stairs, Quint charged toward Jorgie's room. He should have gone to her immediately. If anything bad had happened, he'd never forgive himself. He took the stairs two at a time and burst onto her floor.

The door to her room was closed. Fear knotted his throat.

"Jorgie!" He pounded on the door.

She wrenched the door open so quickly that he tumbled forward and staggered across the threshold. Her eyes were wide, her bottom lip trembling. Her room was trashed. Her clothes strewn about, drawers pulled open, the covers stripped from the bed.

"A ma-man was in my room." She looked pale and shaken.

He grabbed her by the shoulders. "Are you all right?"

She nodded.

"You're sure?"

"Yes."

"Okay, I'm going after him."

"Be careful."

He gave her a quick kiss and then raced back to the lobby. He spun past the crowd, flew out the side door of the resort, and burst out onto the narrow walkway above the canal. He stopped, looked right, then left.

Which way had the intruder gone?

If he went right, the walkway circled back around to the front entrance of the resort. Frank's men, Mario and Gianni, were stationed out there. To avoid them, the intruder had to head left toward the Piazza San Marco, where he could shed his ski mask and quickly be lost among the tourists.

Quint ran toward the piazza, and he spied a black ski mask hanging half out of a trash receptacle. He stopped long enough to grab the mask and stuff it into his back pocket.

The intruder had to be long gone, but he kept running, hoping against hope that somehow he could find the perpetrator. He elbowed aside a pack of teens engaged in horseplay and dodged a man on stilts juggling orange glowing balls. The air was ripe with Sunday-morning-Venice-during-tourist-season smells—fresh baked bread, roasted turkey legs, spicy steak-on-a-stick.

Across the piazza, he saw a man in black moving swiftly through the throng. Was this his quarry?

The years he'd spent in Venice gave him an advantage. The man was headed for a church, aiming to slip through it to the waterway beyond, but Quint knew a shortcut. He turned back the way he'd come, slipping down a narrow side street that exited on the opposite side of the church. Fewer people were here. It was easier to gain ground.

He reached the canal just as the man emerged from the church, heading away from Quint.

Quint poured on the leg power, sprinting as fast as he could.

The intruder wasn't expecting him, but he must have heard Quint's footsteps because he started running, but he was too late.

Like a cheetah bringing down a gazelle. Quint was on him, grabbing the man around the shoulders, taking him to the ground. The force of the momentum sent them both flying, and they stopped on the edge of the street, inches from falling into the canal. Quint drew back his fist, ready to fight if the guy was so inclined.

"Don't hit me, don't hit me." The man raised his hands to shield his face.

Quint stopped. He knew him.

It was Joe Vincent from his Casanova class.

Chapter 18

Quint hauled a handcuffed Joe Vincent back to the resort. They arrived at the front door just as Dougal Lockhart and Taylor Milton disembarked from the vaporetto.

"Here's your saboteur," he said.

Cool as always, Taylor simply raised an eyebrow. "Good work, Mr. Mason."

Everyone went into the lobby, and they were greeted with a chorus of complaints. Several people at the front desk were angry because their rooms had been ransacked. Quint spied Jorgie sitting off to one side, her ashen skin turned his stomach. It was all he could do not to go to her. Her eyes widened when she saw Joe Vincent.

"Give me a second, fellows," Taylor said, and stopped at the desk. "Everyone whose room has been ransacked will get a voucher for a free Eros vacation."

A cheer went up from the disgruntled group.

She nodded to Quint and Dougal and motioned toward her office on the ground floor. "This way."

Quint took Vincent's elbow and guided him after Taylor. He mouthed, "later" to Jorgie as they walked past her.

Jorgie nodded, wide-eyed and scared.

Taylor opened her door, let them all in, then went to take her seat.

"Sit down." Dougal took Joe from Quint and shoved the man into the chair across from Taylor's desk.

Quint told them what had happened.

"You can't prove nothin'." Pouty Joe pouched out his lower lip.

He tried to get to his feet, but Quint planted him back in his chair with a firm hand on the man's shoulder. "We have a witness who caught you coming out of her room. You might as well come clean. You're the one who ransacked the guest rooms."

Taylor leaned back in her chair, steepled her fingertips, and shot the man a steady glare. "Why have you been sabotaging my resorts, Mr. Vincent?"

Joe said nothing.

"This is serious business," she said. "That bomb in Japan could have hurt someone if it had gone off."

"Hey!" Joe snarled. "That wasn't me."

"But the incidents here in Venice?" Taylor waved a hand at their surroundings. "That was you?"

Joe just shrugged.

"And the threatening e-mail?"

He shook his head.

"Who are you working?" Dougal asked. "Why are you doing this?"

Joe said nothing but sweat beaded on his forehead.

"Okay, if you want to go down for someone else's crime, fine by me. I'll call the local police." Dougal picked up the receiver.

"Wait!" Joe looked panicked.

Dougal paused.

"I'm just the hired help," Joe said. "I get instructions, I do what I'm told. I get paid. That's all I know."

"Who hired you?" Taylor got to her feet and splayed her palms on the desk. She looked formidable.

"I want immunity," Joe said. "If I tell you who hired me, then I walk away free."

Dougal looked at Taylor. Quint waited quietly with his hands clasped behind his back.

Taylor nodded and sank back down. "Very well. If you agree to testify against the person who hired you, I won't press charges against you. But I want a name and I want it now."

Joe gulped. "Okay."

"The name?" Taylor crooked her finger in a cough-it-up gesture.

"General Charles Miller."

Taylor blinked as a flicker of surprise passed over her face, but she quickly recovered. "Cut the crap."

"I'm not kidding," Joe said, then he rattled off the times and places he'd been contacted by the general and the things he'd been asked to do. "He hired other people for the other resorts. I was only one of four."

Joe told them everything he'd done to sabotage the resort, including causing the blackout and ransacking the guests' rooms, following Quint and Jorgie to the island and stealing their boat.

Taylor looked completely unsettled. "But why would General Miller do that? He was my father's best friend. He and his wife are my godparents."

"He told me he hated what you'd done to your father's airline. That your old man would be ashamed of you. He wanted to scare you into closing down the resorts. That's all I know."

Taylor slumped in her chair, betrayal in her eyes. She put a hand over her mouth. "I'll need to confirm that."

"Fine by me." Joe said. "It's your turn."

Taylor picked up the phone and made a call. "Hello, Mitzi? It's Taylor. Is Chuck there?" There was a pause. "Yes, I realize it's the middle of the night where you are, but this is important."

A long silence passed. No one said anything inside the room as Taylor waited on the phone connection.

"Chuck," she said, her voice coming out tight. "Sorry to wake you, but I have someone in my office who has leveled a serious accusation against you, and I need to hear your side of the story."

Then calmly, quietly, she told the man she'd trusted like a father what Joe Vincent had just told them.

Another long moment of silence passed in the room. Quint could hear the ticking of the wall clock.

"I see," she said at last. Taylor's entire body shook. "I'm sorry you feel that way and I'm sorry you felt the need to correct me. Your methods were not only hurtful, but they were criminal as well. You can expect a call from my lawyers."

After ending the call, Taylor clenched her jaw and took a second to compose herself. "He confessed."

"Wow," Dougal said. "Just wow."

Taylor pressed her lips together and glanced up at the ceiling to collect herself before continuing. "That man was a general in the U.S. Air Force and he crept around tike a passive-aggressive sneak thief to undermine everything I've tried to build. Unbelievable."

"Come on," Dougal said, moving across the room to put his arm around Taylor's shoulders. "You need to call Daniel. He'll want to catch the next plane out to be with you through this."

Taylor shook her head. "No, I'm not staying. I'm going home to Daniel."

"I'll escort you."

"What do I do with him?" Quint nodded at Joe.

"Leave him to me," Dougal said. "You can go pack your things. Your assignment is over. You've worked hard. Take a couple of weeks off."

"You sure?" Quint asked, but even as he was asking, he was thinking of Jorgie. He couldn't wait to see her again and make sure she was really okay.

"Yes."

"Thank you. Quint," Taylor said. "Well done."

Quint nodded and left the room, feeling awful for her and grateful he didn't have to deal with the details. He hurried down the corridor and through the lobby, bent on getting to Jorgie.

———— ◉ ————

FIVE MINUTES LATER, Quint knocked on Jorgie's door.

She answered, tipping him a slight smile from behind the half-opened door. He recognized the coy courtesan smirk she'd perfected in her class. One look at her and he felt out of whack, as if he might come down with the flu or something.

"Hi," he said.

"Hi, yourself."

"We should talk."

"That sounds serious."

"It is."

Her grin faded.

Quint rested his arm on the door frame and leaned toward her. "Can I come in?"

'The place is still a mess from being ransacked. Housekeeping can't get here for hours."

"1 don't care."

She stepped aside and let him in. He stalked to the middle of the room, stopped, and turned back to look at her.

The woman was a vision and all he wanted to do was touch her, but he couldn't. Not yet. Not until they'd straightened things out between them.

"Have a seat." She pointed to the chair beside the bed.

He sat.

She had a suitcase opened, and it was half-filled with clothes.

"You're packing," he said.

"Yes, we fly home tomorrow morning. I thought that was why you'd come," she said. "To say goodbye and catch me up on what happened."

"No," he said. "I came to tell you the truth. I haven't been completely honest with you."

"Oh?" She tried to look nonchalant, but he could see worry fretting in her beautiful blue eyes. "How's that?"

"I'm not really Casanova."

"I know that."

"That's not what I meant." He noticed she stayed halfway across the room, as if she didn't trust herself around him.

"I'm listening." She crossed her arms over her chest, hunched her shoulders, drawing herself, shielding her body.

She was afraid of getting hurt. He couldn't blame her. He was scared, too.

"I'm not a Casanova expert. I'm not an instructor for Eros. I'm a private duty air marshal on an undercover assignment."

She laughed.

"What's so funny?" He frowned.

"Private duty air marshal?"

"Yes."

She studied him. "You mean it?"

He pulled his wallet from his back pocket, took out his credentials, passed them to her.

She looked at them, her eyes widening, her mouth opening. "For real?"

"For real."

Then he explained to her what he was doing at Eros and why he was posing as an instructor for the Casanova course. He told her about the man who'd ransacked her room and how they'd caught him. How Joe Vincent confessed to stealing their boat and leaving them stranded on the island to create chaos and division at the resort.

After he finished, she said nothing, just sat down on the edge of the bed, arms still crossed over her chest, still shutting him out.

He wanted to go to her, hug her, tell her all this hand nothing to do with her, with them, but she looked so shutdown, so unapproachable.

"That's terrible. It's got to be such a shock for Taylor. Finding out the man she trusted, her godfather, would betray her like that."

"Taylor's tough and she's a great husband, and a got a lot of good friends. She'll survive."

Jorgie took a deep breath, rubbed her palms along her upper thighs. She was wearing black workout pants, and they clung to her curvy thighs. "Why are you telling me all this?"

"Because I wanted to be honest with you. I couldn't tell you before because of my job, but I wanted you to know."

"You didn't need to do that. I'll be gone tomorrow, and we'll probably never see each other ever again."

"I want us to keep going after this. I want to date and see where this leads," he said, putting all his cards on the table.

She shook her head.

"No?" His throat constricted.

"I don't think that's a good idea." She stood up, picked up a pair of slacks that were lying on the bed. She folded them up and tucked them in the suitcase.

He felt panicky. The way he'd in college when he'd overslept after partying too hard and missed his math final his senior year. He'd been terrified his professor would not let him take a make-up exam, but he'd given the instructor his patented Mason grin and she'd relented. He tried that grin now with Jorgie.

"Let's talk this through."

"There's nothing to talk about. I knew when we had sex that I would lose you. You're only fascinated with me because I'm telling you it's over. That this is goodbye."

"That's not true!" Was it? No one had ever dumped him before. In the past, his relationships are parted amicable for both sides, or he'd been the one to break off the relationship, usually just before things started getting serious.

"Honestly, a relationship with you would be too exhausting. Playing games is fun, but at some point you have to put the fantasies aside and get on with real life. You've never left the playground. Quint. And that's okay. It's who you are. I accept it. That's why I'm saying goodbye."

She spoke lightly, matter-of-factly, but he knew he'd hurt her, and it killed him to think he'd caused her pain.

He rubbed his jaw. "Jorgie, I'm sorry. I never—"

"Don't apologize," she said, "That's like a zebra apologizing his stripes. I knew what I was getting into. I accept that this affair was temporary."

"Jorgie," he said her name softly, gave her his most coaxing grin. "I want to continue this relationship. I want *you*."

But she wasn't listening. She was stuffing clothes, panties, bras, socks, and tops in the suitcase. He felt invisible.

"Jorgie..." He was wheedling now, trying to negotiate for a position of powerlessness. He moved toward her with a hand outstretched.

She dropped the shirt she was holding. "No, just no. You stop right there."

He wanted to touch her more than anything in the world, but he respected her boundaries and stopped, even though he kept reaching for her. "Jorgie."

"Please, don't touch me—" Her eyes flooded with tears. "I couldn't bear it if you touch me."

"I have to fix this. How can I fix this? I can't let you slip through my fingers."

"Look, this was all wrong from the start. I thought I wanted casual sex, but in my heart I knew I wasn't a woman who could take intimacy lightly. I listened to my friend Avery, and I listened to my hormones, and I listened to Maggie Cantrell telling me how to be a courtesan, but I didn't listen to my gut that was telling me not to sleep with you and now I have to pay the price. But it's my price to pay."

"But why? Why can't we just be together?"

"Because Casanova never changed."

"Huh?" He blinked.

"Casanova spent his whole life chasing the thrill of romantic love. He went through crush after crush, infatuation after infatuation, but in the end he was disappointed by all his relationships."

"Not his relationship with Lady Evangeline."

"That's because she never gave in to him. They never had sex. They didn't end up together. Quint."

He fisted his hands, swallowed hard. He could feel himself losing her. "I'm not Casanova."

"Aren't you?"

"Absolutely not."

"You flit from one relationship to the other, avoiding commitment..."

"I wasn't avoiding commitment."

"Then what do you call it?"

"I was waiting." He leveled a gaze at her.

"Waiting?"

"For the right one to come along."

She laughed, but it was a tight, mirthless sound. "How many women have you said that to?"

"None. Zero. You're the only one."

"You only want me because I'm ending things."

"That's not true."

"It's okay, Quint. I don't blame you. I learned a lot about myself, and I had fun. It's enough."

"It's not enough for me!"

"You'll survive. I'm sure many women at this villa would be happy to take my place."

"I don't want them. I want you."

She went to the door, opened it, and stood to one side, her eyes begging him to leave. "You can't always get what you want."

He went to her, took the door from her hand, shut it. "Jorgie, please, reconsider."

She closed her eyes, then took a long, deep breath. Her hand was trembling. Then she opened her eyes and shot him a look of abject sorrow. Her fragile vulnerability knifed him in the gut. Without ever intending to do, he'd cut her to the quick.

"Jorgie," he whispered, and pressed his back against the door. "Are you saying if I showed up on your front porch when we get back home that you'd send me away?"

She glanced up, and he saw tears shimmer in her eyes. "You know I wouldn't possess the courage to turn you away. Not when you're wearing that charming smile and saying sweet things like you're saying right now."

"See there," he said. "See right there? That means we've got something special."

"All I see is a woman too bowled over by a handsome man to get out while she had a shred of dignity intact." She pushed her hair back from her face with both hands. "Will you just go?"

"Jorgie, please. We can work through this. I know there's a solution."

"Yes, you go your way and I go mine and we simply enjoy what we had and tuck it away as nothing more than a sweet memory."

"I want more, and I think you do, too."

"There can't be more. This was all a sweet fantasy. It was just a dream. Our relationship won't stand up to the pressure of normal life. If you were honest about yourself, you'd admit it. Now, please, just go."

He couldn't swallow past the lump clogging his throat.

She stood there, not saying another word, and for one small second his heart surged with hope. Maybe she was reconsidering?

"I'm such an idiot," she whispered. "I told myself I could do this, Quint. That I could play games and have fun and keep my heart out of it. I kept telling myself what I was feeling was nothing more than an enjoyable time with an old friend and you were like a soothing balm on a raw wound of my last relationship. I knew our tryst was for two weeks and nothing longer." She paused, hitched in a breath, swiped at the tears trickling down her face. "I would appreciate it if you'd leave now."

If that was what she wanted, he had no choice but to honor it. He stepped into the hallway, and she shut the door behind him.

Quint stood silently, cut to the bone by her comment and seared by the swell of his own shame. Dazed, he walked down the corridor, shoving his hands in his pockets. How had this happened? The last thing on earth he'd ever wanted to do was hurt Jorgie. The thought of it sliced his soul. He'd partied his way through life thinking that if he embraced good times, had fun, he could avoid pain.

Now this woman had shown him how wrong he'd been about himself, about life. It killed him to lose her. Absolutely laid him low and shoved him in a pit of despair.

And that's when Quint knew, beyond any doubt, he'd fallen in love with Jorgie Gerard.

Chapter 19

Not knowing what else to do, Quint went back to his room. He'd never felt like this, and he didn't know how to handle his overwhelming sadness.

He paced, trying to come up with some kind of plan to win Jorgie over. But was he wrong to do so? If she didn't want to be pursued, shouldn't he leave her alone? If he really loved her, wouldn't he accept that she didn't want him and wish for her a happy life filled with love, even if he couldn't be the one to give her that love?

Yes, yes, he should.

The masculine side of him urged him to fight for her. Told him she was worth fighting for. But he would not make her feel scared or unsafe around him. He had to accept her request. He had no real option, no matter how much he wanted to be with her.

A knock sounded on his door.

Quint jumped. Could it possibly be Jorgie?

He yanked opened the door without looking through the peephole, only to have his hopes dashed.

"May I come in?" Dougal asked.

"Sure, sure." Quint stepped aside and ushered his boss inside.

"You okay?" Dougal narrowed his eyes at him. "You look..." He paused, studied him. "Shook up. This whole thing with Taylor and General Miller got you that upset?"

"It is troubling." Quint wasn't ready to confess about Jorgie. It was none of Dougal's business. "I still can't believe her godfather was behind the threats."

"Disturbing." Dougal nodded. "I've called our men at the other resorts and notified law enforcement."

"What about Joe Vincent?"

"Taylor promised him she wouldn't prosecute, so we let him go."

"And Miller?"

Dougal shook his head, sank down in the chair at the desk, leaned back. "That's between him and Taylor. Our job is done."

'The general must have had a serious moral conflict with Taylor over what direction she took her father's airline. You'd think he could have simply told her how he felt."

"It was more than that. He was on the board of directors and Taylor believes he's been embezzling from her, as well. She's got her legal team looking into it. Apparently, he was using the sabotage as a coverup, keep her attention elsewhere while he funneled money to an account in the Caymans."

"Ah, money and greed. A motive you can count on?"

"So," Dougal said, "you're free from Casanova."

"And you get to go home to Roxie."

"I can't wait to see my fiancée. From now on I'm sticking to running the office. Let you single guys take to the air." Dougal looked so happy about it.

Quint was jealous of Dougal's peace of mine. "You sure you won't miss flying?"

"Been there, done that, have much better things to do now. Are sure you're all right? You look pretty down. I've never seen you so hangdog. Did something happen with your friend who played Lady Evangeline?"

"Yeah, it was the darndest thing." Quint experienced a hot tightening in his heart.

"What's that?"

"I fell in love." Speaking the words out loud to another human being made it real.

Dead silence fell in the room. Dougal blinked at him and then grinned. "For a minute there, I thought you said you fell in love."

"I did."

Dougal laugh filled the room.

"I'm serious. Why are you laughing?"

"You've always scoffed at marriage. At even living with a woman. You pride yourself on being footloose and fancy-free. Hell, you've never had a relationship that lasted longer than a few months."

Quint sat down hard on the bed. "What can I say? I was blind, but now I see. Trouble is, she doesn't believe me. She sees me as a Casanova. She won't give me a chance to prove myself to her."

"So, what are you going to do?"

"That's what you're supposed to tell me. You've been down this road. You're my boss. Give me some guidance."

"Are you saying you want to marry this woman?"

"Yeah, I think I am."

Dougal's smile broke across his face. He got up to pound Quint on the shoulder. "That's wonderful. Congratulations."

"There's just one big problem."

"What's that?"

"She doesn't want to see me again."

He thought of going forward without Jorgie in his life. Flying on planes from one city to another, never in any place long enough to catch his breath. How had he ever thought that nomad life was superior to the one most people were living?

A loving, stable life filled with family and friends. His own life felt so hollow now.

Quint remembered how happy his brother Gordy had looked with his wife and kids when he'd gone to visit them. He thought about his old friend Keith, Jorgie's brother. He was married now, with a baby on the way. He saw how narrow his world was compared to what they had. For the first time in his life, he felt left out.

In a few months, he'd be thirty. How long was he going to play Peter Pan? He'd look pretty pathetic at forty-five partying with young things on his arm. How long could a guy hang on his youth without looking like a fool?

These past two weeks with Jorgie had shown him how wonderful the future could be if he'd just open his mind and his heart to a world full of new possibilities. She was a woman who would be his friend and his lover. She balanced him in a way he'd never been balanced. She was smart and funny and pretty and grounded. She was the yin to his yang.

And he would not let her walk away without a fight.

"Dougal," he said, "I need your help."

———◦———

JORGIE BOARDED the Eros plane bound for Texas with a heavy heart. *Just keep putting one foot in front of the other. You'll get through this. You'll get over Quint..*

It sounded like a game plan, but she did not know how to make it happen. How did you begin to forget the love of your life?

She couldn't wait to see Avery again. Avery would know what to do. Avery had been snapping her out of funks since they were five years old.

This is more than just a funk and you know it.

She stowed her luggage, sat down, and bent to stuff her purse underneath the seat in front of her. As she did, something slipped out of her bag.

A little red glass cat.

The minute she saw it, she lost her composure, and felt tears push against her eyelids. She curled her fingers around the cat and clutched it to her heart. *Dammit.*

Why had she broken things off with Quint? Why had she been so shortsighted?

But she'd had to break up with him. She'd had no choice. It was better to leave him before he left her. Because eventually, he would leave her. She wasn't enough for a man like Quint.

Sighing, she leaned back against the headrest, closed her eyes, swallowed hard and prayed Quint would not be on this flight. He'd told her he had things to settle with his undercover work at Eros and she hoped that meant he'd have to stay longer, and she could avoid him.

She heard the doors close and felt the plane taxi toward the runway. Once they were airborne, she let out her breath and loosened her grip on the little glass cat.

Okay. Quint wasn't onboard. She could survive this as long as he respected her wishes to stay away. Eventually, she'd get over him.

"Miss Gerard?"

Jorgie looked up to see the flight attendant smiling down at her.

"Yes?"

"Could you come with me, please?"

"What is it?"

The flight attendant looked around at the other passengers. "I need to speak to you in private, if that's okay."

"Yes, all right." What was this about? She unbuckled her seat belt, settled the little glass cat down on her vacated seat, and followed the flight attendant to the back of the plane.

"Please step behind the divider." The flight attendant waved at the accordion door that cordoned off a small alcove area of the lavish private jet.

"I don't understand. What's this about?"

"Please." The flight attendant just smiled and waited.

With a sigh, Jorgie pushed aside the accordion door and stepped into the alcove.

"Hello, Little Bit," Quint said.

Her heart started thumped so loud she couldn't hear anything else. If she were smart, she would turn right around, go back to her seat, buckle herself in and refuse to move for the rest of the flight, but one look in his cocoa-colored eyes and she was a goner.

"Quint," she said. "What's this about?"

"I quit my job."

"What? Why?"

"I don't want to be on the road anymore. I'm tired of the flying, of my crazy lifestyle. I'm ready to settle down and you're the one I want to do it with."

"How can you know that?"

He touched his chest right over his heart. "I feel it, deep down in here. I'm willing to take things as slowly as you want. I'm willing to wait. I just had to let you know how I feel. If you don't feel the same, I understand and I'll back off, but I couldn't let you go without telling you. I love you, Jorgie."

She wanted to explain that she felt the same way too, but she was so afraid of getting hurt even more than she was already hurting.

"I don't get it. You could have any woman you wanted," she said. "Why me?"

"Besides the fact that I'm madly in love with you?"

"Are you?"

He took her into his arms and kissed her, and she let him. Encouraged him by kissing him back.

"Does that answer your question?" he asked.

"It's just a kiss, Casanova."

"No." He shook his head. "No more Casanova."

"How can you give up your lifestyle just like that?"

"Because I've found something far better."

"Another job?"

"Actually, yes. I've been thinking I might like to be a teacher for real. Not teaching sex tips, of course, but I want to go back to college and get certified to teach high school."

"Really?" Her knees wobbled. How she hoped he meant it.

"Really. You've changed me, Jorgie. I know it's fast. I know I'll have to prove it to you, but I'm willing to try if you are?"

"I-I..." All her dreams were in front of her. All she had to do was give Quint a chance.

"Love's a powerful force. It can change minds and melt hearts." He pulled her closer, nuzzled her neck.

"Why do you love me?"

"I love you because you keep me guessing. I love you because you're both strong and sexy and vulnerable and sweet. I love you because you see right through me. You're able to see the *real* me underneath all the fast talking and fun-loving antics I hide behind. You saw the real me and yet you still liked me."

"Not just *like* you... I love you."

"You do?" He looked so vulnerable she almost burst out laughing.

"I do."

"But why do you love me? What is there about me for a woman like you to love?"

What? Was he blind to his own good qualities?

"Are you really that unaware of what you offer?" she asked.

"Well..." He shrugged. "I've been told I'm not bad in bed, but that doesn't make me husband material."

"That's just a skill. It's not who you are."

"I've never had a long-term relationship."

"By your own choice." She traced his bottom lip with her index finger. "Besides, there's a first time for everything."

"You're not afraid I'll let you down?"

"You could never let me down, Quint."

"Really? Because here I am, a guy who's spent his life having fun and playing games and running away from responsibility."

"You didn't run from responsibility when it counted," she said. "You were in the Air Force. That takes commitment. And when that saboteur knocked me down, you were right by my side when you should have gone after him straight away."

"I had to make sure you were all right."

"Yes, you love to have fun, but when it comes down to it, you've got the ability to face circumstances head-on. You're fully engaged with life, and I need that to shake me out of my staid little one-track existence. You focus on the world of possibilities, and that's exciting to a literal-minded accountant like me. You're a joy to be with and you make me smile. A lot."

He swallowed. "You believe in me that much?"

"I do. My love is here to stay. It's not written in invisible ink. It won't disappear if you make me mad. I love you for who you are. Quint. All sides of you. The good, the bad and the myriad in between. None of us are perfect. We all stumble and fall, but when you have someone who loves you to pick you up and dust you off, getting back up is easy."

"Jorgie." He drew her into his arms. "You're amazing."

"No more so than you." She stared into his mahogany brown eyes and what she saw reflected in those depths moved her deeply.

She had no doubts about him or their future. None. On the surface they might be opposites—a fun- loving, impulsive man and a cautious, practical woman. But underneath it all, where it really counted, they valued the same things—romance, equanimity, tranquility. Quint provided the stimulation, and she was his audience. She'd balance the books, and he'd make sure she didn't get too caught up in the details.

As their mouths joined again, she thought of how she'd loved since she was thirteen. How he'd always been her dream man.

Now the dream was coming true. She'd found the courage to spin the bottle, play the game, and she'd won.

Fun and games had led them here. To the deepest intimacy of their lives.

And when he slipped his palm up underneath her shirt and asked if she was game to join the mile-high club, Jorgie knew the fun had just begun.

Epilogue

As the sun set over the small town of Everly, Texas, Quint stood on the porch of the farmhouse he and Jorgie had just finished renovating. Once Quint had finished his certification to teach high school history, he'd proposed to Jorgie and they'd gotten married and moved the lovely little village, not too far from the town where Jorgie had grown up. Her brother, Keith, had been his best man and Jorgie's best friend Avery had been her matron of honor.

It had been two years since Quint left Eros Airlines and the fast-paced, high-pressure world of air marshalling to put down roots with the love of his life.

And oh what a life it had turned out to be. Quint had connected with old friends and strengthened his bond with his family. He loved teaching as much as he thought he would and didn't miss his old lifestyle, not for a second. He'd grown and changed and moved on. Now, he was building a life on the farm with the wife he adored.

It felt so good to belong somewhere. Belong to somebody. He didn't know why he'd resisted falling in love so hard.

From the day he and Jorgie had joined the mile high club on the plane, they'd been inseparable. They spent their days working side by side on the farm, except during tax season when Jorgie was snowed with her CPA business. They laughed and joked as they tended to the animals and their crops. And at night, they would curl up together on the couch, watching movie or reading books, their bodies intertwined as they discussed their hopes and dreams for the future. Lately, they'd been talking a lot about babies.

It hadn't always been easy, of course. There had been moments where Jorgie had questioned whether Quint really was ready for commitment, whether he could really let go of the excitement of his old way of life and embrace the easy simplicity of the farm. But every time she voiced her doubts, he'd been there to reassure her, to hold her close and tell her she had nothing to fear. He loved her mother than life itself.

With each passing day, Quint become more and more certain that he'd found his true soulmate in Jorgie. She was kind and patient and selfless, and he did his best to put her needs ahead of his. And when they disagree, as all couples do, they never lost sight of the love that bound together.

He heard the door snap closed behind him and turned to find Jorgie standing there with a shy smile on her face.

"Hey there, beautiful," he said. "How was your day?"

Jorgie's smile widened and she came closer, he hands hidden behind her back. "It was good." Her eyes sparkled. "But I have some news."

Quint raised an eyebrow. "What news?"

Jorgie took a deep breath and held out her hands, revealing a small white stick. It took him a second to recognize what she was holding.

"A-are you...?" Quint stopped breathing, waiting.

"I'm pregnant," she whispered.

For a moment, Quint stood frozen in shock. They'd talked about babies, sure, but he hadn't expected this to happen so soon.

"How do you feel?" She nibbled her bottom lip, gauging his reaction.

"I feel amazing!" He pulled Jorgie into a tight hug. "We're having a baby!"

Jorgie laughed and hugged him back, her face buried against his chest as she squeezed him as hard as she could.

As they pulled apart, Quint took her hand and led her over to the porch swing and sat down next to her. He gazed deeply into her eyes, feeling a keen sense of love and gratitude wash over him.

"You're going to be an incredible mother," he said, overcome by emotions.

"And you'll be such a fun dad."

They sat there in the dwindling twilight, holding each other and dreaming about their future as a family. The entire world felt wide open. Deep contentment took hold of him, and he knew that with Jorgie by his side, he was up for this adventure of a lifetime.

As the crickets started to chirping and the air filled with the flicker of lightning bugs, they sat wrapped up in their love for each other and the new life growing inside of Jorgie. They key that whatever might come, they would face it together, with love and strength and commitment. And with their little on the way, their love would only grow deeper every day.

Don't miss out!

Visit the website below and you can sign up to receive emails whenever Lori Wilde publishes a new book. There's no charge and no obligation.

https://books2read.com/r/B-A-BAEH-JIKFC

BOOKS 2 READ

Connecting independent readers to independent writers.

Did you love *Mr. Undeniable*? Then you should read *Mr. Temptation*[1] by Lori Wilde!

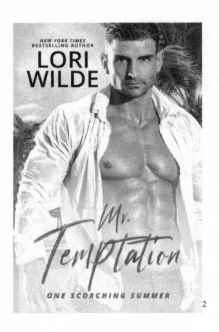

Are you looking for a steamy read to spice up your night? Look no further than Mr. Temptation by NYT bestselling author, Lori Wilde. When handsome Coast Guard Lieutenant Commander, Scott Everly, goes undercover to catch a drug smuggling kingpin, he clashes with sexy biologist, Jackie Birchard, who is striving to save a rare species in the Florida Keys. Sparks fly as they must work together to stop the smugglers. With plot twists and surprises at every turn, this novel will ignite a passion that can't be denied. Get ready for

---

1. https://books2read.com/u/bPNyzl

2. https://books2read.com/u/bPNyzl

some serious heat with sexy scenes that won't disappoint! You won't want to put this book down until you reach its explosive conclusion. This steamy, standalone romantic suspense will keep you turning the pages.

Read more at https://loriwilde.com.

Also by Lori Wilde

Cowboy Confidential
Cowboy Cop
Cowboy Protector
Cowboy Bounty Hunter
Cowboy Bodyguard
Cowboy Outlaw

Cowboy Country
Arizona Heat

Cowboy Rendezvous
Tomaz
Jake
Cody

Heartthrob Hospital

The Thunderbolt
The Jinx
The Hotshot

Kringle, Texas
A Perfect Christmas Gift
A Perfect Christmas Wish
A Perfect Christmas Surprise
A Perfect Christmas Joy
A Perfect Christmas Reunion

One Scorching Summer
Mr. Temptation
Mr. Temptation
Mr. Intoxicating
Mr. Undeniable
Mr. Scandalous

Texas Rascals
Keegan
Matt
Kurt
Tucker
Kael
Brodie
Dan

Rex

Clay

Jonah

Watch for more at https://loriwilde.com.

About the Author

Lori Wilde is the New York Times, USA Today and Publishers' Weekly bestselling author of 85 works of romantic fiction. She's a three time Romance Writers' of America RITA finalist and has four times been nominated for Romantic Times Readers' Choice Award. She has won numerous other awards as well. Her books have been translated into 26 languages, with more than four million copies of her books sold worldwide. Her breakout novel, The First Love Cookie Club, has been optioned for a TV movie.

Lori is a registered nurse with a BSN from Texas Christian University. She holds a certificate in forensics, and is also a certified yoga instructor.

A fifth generation Texan, Lori lives with her husband, Bill, in the Cutting Horse Capital of the World; where they run

Epiphany Orchards, a writing/creativity retreat for the care and enrichment of the artistic soul.

Read more at https://loriwilde.com.